SECRET CHOICES

Tom Puetz

First Edition

ISBN 978-0-9892060-0-6
eISBN 978-0-9892060-1-3

Dragon Tale Books, LLC
http://dragontalebooks.com

This book is a work of fiction. Names, characters, places, and incidents either are products of the author's imagination or are used fictitiously. Any resemblance to actual persons, living or dead, events, or locales is entirely coincidental.

Acknowledgements

I greatly appreciate, and sincerely thank these friends:
Tom Bird – for teaching me how to connect deeply and write from the heart. He saved my life.

Brad Lukey – for his encouragement and motivation, even when I didn't want it.

Karen McClain Kiefer – for her professional assistance and friendship.

Lori Shupp – for discovering the promise of this book and for all the phrases I *borrowed* from her.

* * *

This work is dedicated
to those who carry the pride and the shame
of being a good soldier.

* * *

Contents

I am Cold, Numb.

There was a war. I killed a man.
And then
There was a great love. I let her go.
And now
I listen for my heartbeat.

I am Cold, Numb.

Class Reunion

Saturday, June 22nd, 1984: Freeland, Indiana

"Did you kill anybody?" Jim asked.

"Yes. Yes, I did," Tom answered, then looked away.

Tom Warden was back in Indiana for his twentieth high school reunion. He was drinking with his classmate, Jim, who was still farming, not like most of Tom's friends. When Jim asked, *Did you kill anybody*? the question jerked Tom back. Vietnam was fifteen years in his past and not in the news anymore, but it was front page in Tom's mind more often than he liked.

Jim said, "I didn't think ya had it in ya, Tom."

"Well, I guess I didn't when you knew me."

"You were just a quiet guy, kinda cautious." Jim took a swallow of beer, and placed the bottle on the bar.

Tom spoke to the beer bottle. "One day I just had to pull the trigger. Had to kill." *Bullshit*, came the voice in Tom's mind, *You didn't have to*. He straightened his posture, turned to Jim and said, "You know I was drafted."

"The Army?"

"Yeah, the Army…an infantry sergeant."

"A sarge. Hell, Tom, I can't picture you as a sergeant."

"Yeah, well, me neither. I actually volunteered for special training to get my sergeant stripes."

"Hey, drink another beer for Sgt. Warden!" Jim announced to the bar in general.

This was still the only bar in the one-stoplight town of Freeland, Indiana. *Shit, it's been 20 years*. He saw some of the same old faces. There were also some new, but still familiar faces. The sons and daughters of the people he grew up with. The voice in Tom's head rambled on, *I'm glad I don't have sons and daughters. I'm afraid they'd ask me, What did you do in the war, Daddy? Then I'd have to tell them I killed people. You see darling, they wanted a body count. So...I just killed as many people as I could. I even killed some little girls like you...accidentally of course.*

The clatter and chatter of the bar gave him some anonymity, some cover so he wouldn't be noticed, wouldn't have to talk. He listened to his classmates tell stories about their lives since he'd seen them last. Tom didn't have much to tell. He imagined how that conversation would go.

Do you have kids, Tom?
No.
A job?
About twenty since I saw you last.
Prospects?
No, none.
Sweetheart?
Not really.
What do you do?
I just drift and skim life.

Paul walked up and asked Jim if he was ready to start cultivating corn. Jim and Paul drifted down the bar and slid into a booth. Tom spotted Murphy standing against the wall near the booth. He was brushing the floor with the toe of one shoe as if he was looking for something in the dust. Murphy was one of Tom's friends from back in the day. They had played chess all through high school.

Tom walked over to him and said, "Murphy. Hey, how you been?"

Murphy stared at Tom and shook his head. "What? Oh, hey Tom. It's been a few years." He inspected Tom's face.

"You look a little spaced out. You OK?"

Murphy looked at the floor. "Yeah." Then back at Tom. "I saw you come in and started flashing back when..."

"Oh yeah, that's right, you did a tour of duty, too, didn't you?"

"Yeah. Graves registration. I logged the names."

"You didn't see my name there, did you?"

"No, Tom. I didn't see your name. I watched for it, though. I saw the names of some people I knew. Wondered why they died. Still wonder why."

"Jesus, Murphy, don't do that."

Murphy looked up at Tom. "Well, glad to see you made it back."

"Yeah, thanks."

"You didn't really make it back, did you, Tom?"

"No, I guess not. I just feel…like a ghost. How about you?"

"I don't like to explain. Just let it rest. No use, anyway. People care, but they have no understanding. Not really."

Tom looked at the floor. "No, not really. Just let it be." Then he looked up, "You married, Murphy?"

"No."

"Me neither. Not even close. And don't intend to."

The bar held about twenty, packed, and it was. The wooden floor smelled like beer. The same Budweiser neon hung over the jukebox, which was playing "What Kind of Fool am I", *To ever go to war* Tom was thinking as he took a half step closer to Murphy. They were men apart in a room full of revelers. They didn't face each other. They edged to the wall between the booth and window, turned slightly out, watched the crowd as they spoke.

"You missed Tet Offensive, right, Tom?"

"Yeah. I was in boot camp February of '68. I was hoping I might get sent to Germany or Korea, but after Tet, I knew we were all going to Nam. The training seemed different the next day. We were more intense. Paid more attention, like our lives depended on the training."

"I heard Jim say he didn't think you had it in you. I don't think you had it in you, Tom."

"Yeah, I guess not. Maybe it was just the Army training. At first I resisted, tried not to change. Then when I knew I was going into combat in Vietnam, things changed. I wanted to learn how to fight. That's what I told myself, but deep down I wanted to learn how to kill. I wanted to be able to pull the trigger if I needed to. I wanted to see if I had it in me. I was afraid I didn't, so I tried harder. I didn't like being afraid. I figured if I survived combat, I would never be afraid of anything again." Tom looked through the ceiling for a moment, searched Murphy's face. "After advanced infantry training, I volunteered for noncommissioned officer training. 'Shake-n-bake sergeants' they called us. I can't believe I volunteered for special training so I could kill more efficiently. Like…I think I kept telling myself I was training so I could stay alive, but staying alive meant killing. No question. None at all. You know, I even liked the idea that I would be among the elite, one of the men who knew he could kill without hesitation or remorse. I'm ashamed and proud, or neither. Don't know which is real." Tom looked away, his eyes pleading for some distraction.

Murphy kept his eyes on Tom and said, "Don't beat yourself up. I've probably thought about this every day for fifteen years, and I can only say one thing. We had to go. We had to."

"Yeah, we did. We had to go or give up our lives as we knew them by going to Canada or Mexico. What we didn't know is that we would give up our lives anyway. Some literally, some like you and me whose lives are just not the same because of Nam. Why didn't they tell us we would never be the same?"

"Hell, Tom, most of them didn't know what war would do. How could they have known war would make us strangers to ourselves? Some of them knew, I guess."

"Yeah. My mother tried to tell me. She told me about my uncles that were in World War II and said it had changed them. Really changed them. I believed her, but I *wanted* a change. Now I complain and say, *Why didn't somebody tell me?* I guess I wasn't ready for the kind of change it would be. Mom watched me when I got back. Tried to get me help, but I wanted to be the stoic warrior. To be strong, unwavering in my sacrifice. I wanted to be honored for what I did there. I'm ashamed of some of it…try to hide it. I can't bear the thought of telling someone about it. Like, say, what if I was married and it was parents' day? I could show pictures of bodies and burned villages. A day at work with daddy."

"Jesus, Tom, stop. Fuck that. You're going to drive yourself nuts."

"Going to? Going to?"

"OK, Tom, OK. Can you stop it?"

"Well, no. I guess not, but I just can't talk about it with anyone but other vets and then only if they get off on beating themselves up."

"Jesus, Tom. I mean, it's OK to talk about Nam, but you're making stuff up. You don't have kids. You're not in front of a bunch of innocent children explaining war or why you killed people."

"Yes, but most everybody I know is an innocent. They don't know what it was like. They don't know what we had to do to survive."

"I can't change that for you; that's the way it was. Maybe it's better like this. Maybe it wouldn't be healthy for us to just be with vets. We would feel normal. Like it's OK to be jacked up all the time. We would understand each other, but I don't think we would be any happier, any better off. We would just not feel out of place."

Tom just stared at Murphy for a bit. Then he looked out across the bar, checking each person, then back at Murphy. He inched back toward the wall a little behind Murphy. Murphy examined his bottle of beer like he'd never seen one before and drank some. They looked out at the room.

Jim, sitting in the booth, was looking at them. He frowned and said, "Hey, what ya doing? Come on, pull a chair over. Come say hi to Stella."

The room swung around Tom and drew him back to reality. Stella came over and gave Tom a big hug.

"I hate to mention it, but how is your granddaughter?"

"Christ," she said, "I can't believe it. Six months old and just like me."

"As in, she drinks beer and gives good head?" Murphy said.

"Screw you, Murphy. You wish."

"In my dreams. Really, I dream about that."

Tom chuckled. *Yeah, we all wanted head from Stella.* Another thought chased the first one, *Who the hell would name their daughter Stella? Not me.* Another voice in Tom's head told him *You don't have, and never will have a daughter, asshole.*

"You ever get married, Tom?" Stella asked.

"Me? No."

Stella frowned. “I’ll bet you don’t have a girlfriend; do you?”

“Yes I do.”

“Well, Tom, you the have a look of a single guy without a girlfriend.”

“I’m not gay, if that’s what you are saying.”

“Ha. Hey everybody. Tom’s not gay!”

“Bullshit!” someone yelled.

“What about that night at Indiana Beach?” Dan said.

Jim said, “Or should we say the morning after? You and Harv were asleep in the back of his ‘56 Chevy when we found you.”

“That wasn’t Harv. That was Dan. What was that all about?”

“We were so drunk the sheep got away, so we finished the blackberry brandy and passed out.” Tom turned back to Stella. God, we were wasted. You were dating Randy then, weren’t you?”

“Yeah, the love of my life.”

“I never thought you’d break up.”

“Me either. People change though. Or maybe we just got to know each other better. Anyway, twenty years is long enough to have kids and raise them.” Stella watched her cousin stagger out of the bar. She turned back to Tom. “Where does it all end up anyway?” She paid her tab and left.

Tom sat down in the booth and listened to Jim tell about the time he wrecked his dad’s Harley. Tom didn’t say a word the rest of the night. The crowd thinned. People drifted out. Murphy had left with Stella to give her a ride home. She was pretty drunk. *A drunk grandmother.* He would never look at grandmothers the same.

He could see the barroom clearly now. Not a room packed with friends, but a place set up for drinking. A bar stocked with the liquor of your choice. Tables packed close together. It was a drinking machine, but people loved it here. It was a comfort, a place where they could loosen the grip of society with booze and be themselves. The room seemed too bright. Harold was putting the chairs on the tables. They had run out of Miller.

Harold looks the same age he did the first time I came in here. Well, he was about ten years older than me then, and he still is ten years older than me. Why did I leave before I saw this place for what it was? A place to get drunk and act and think like you wished you could all week.

Tom got up and went to piss. He read the graffiti over the urinal. "This is where Napoleon beat his bone-apart." His thoughts ran on.

Same thing I saw here 20 years ago. Still smells the same, beer with a hint of vomit. Christ, no chance for change here. No reprieve. No answers. Except for Murphy. He understands. He figured it out. He accepted this in his hometown. Why isn't it my hometown?

Tom wanted a hometown. He wished he could just come back here and have things be the way they used to be. *No way, too many real images, not enough mystery.*

Tom went back out into the bar. Jim and some guy Tom didn't know were talking together in the booth. Tom turned and walked out to his pickup, which was parked across the street in the feed store parking lot. Tom remembered seeing his first movie there on the side of the three-story building. The movie was *Snow White and the Seven Dwarfs*, a fairytale. He looked at the grey weathered wall of the feed store and said out loud, "I wish I could live in a fairy tale."

He got in his '67 Ford pickup and lit a cigarette.

Where to go? I could visit my sister in Fowler or drive back to Massachusetts. Or I could drive to Alabama and find Ted.

He started the pickup and drove out of town the way he did back in the day, toward the farm where he grew up. It was dark. No one around to suggest anything was different than what it ever was. For a moment he wished the sun would never come up and he could drive in the night forever. It felt right. He drove, hardly thinking.

He passed the farmhouse where he grew up. His mom and dad had sold the farm and moved to Arizona. The house was empty. He stopped at the corner one quarter of a mile down the gravel road, then turned around, and went back. He turned into the lane as if he still lived there and let the pickup roll to a stop beside the windmill. A quarter moon gave some light. He could see the corn would be knee high by the fourth of July. He lit another cigarette and sat in his pickup beside the empty farmhouse. As he was falling asleep he thought of Ted, his childhood friend and neighbor. In the morning he would make the mile-and-a-half drive to the farm where Ted grew up to see if he had made it back from Alabama for the class reunion.

Prisoner of War

Monday December 15th, 1968: En route to the Republic of South Vietnam

The plane had been refueled in Alaska. Tom Warden had been watching the time and verified that he and the aircraft had passed the point of no return. His being on an airplane carrying troops to South Vietnam was not an accident or some twist of fate. Tom had made definite choices. He could have avoided the draft and gone to Canada. He could have been a conscientious objector. He could have joined the Navy and stayed out of the infantry. He could have committed a felony and spent time in jail instead of Vietnam. He chose to drop out of college, allow himself to be drafted, be trained as a soldier, and sent to Vietnam. Even now, past the point of no return, the reasons for those choices were not clear to him. He told himself it didn't make any difference; then he was overwhelmed by the feeling that it made all the difference in the world.

It was in the fall of 1967 when Tom started making clear decisions about his future. A certain dissatisfaction with life had overtaken him. He wondered if an ordinary life was worth living. When he thought about the daily grind of a regular job, the promise of a family living in a nice house complete with front porch and white picket fence, it seemed like giving up. Tom wanted more but had no idea what that life could be. He had not made enough money that summer to pay for a full year at Purdue University. He did not like the carpentry work he was good at, and it was hard to find a part-time job as a carpenter that would carry him through the spring semester. One very clear option was to drop out of college and be drafted. The truth was, sometimes he was not certain if he wanted to go on living or not. He knew that if he was a soldier in Vietnam, he would either fight for his life—or he would not. He was sure that if he didn't, he would die there. He was sure that if he did whatever it took to survive, he would be able to live the rest of his life with courage and conviction.

Three of his uncles were World War II veterans, but it never occurred to Tom to ask them about war. They never talked about it so Tom didn't see them as war veterans. He never thought of them as having been soldiers in a war. His image of war, and the men who fought them, came from the movies and television. The strange part was that, to Tom, soldiers and heroes were more like characters from myth and legend. Not people you could talk to. The idea that he could actually *be* a soldier, *become* one of those men, was intoxicating. He wanted to be like Audie Murphy, a war hero of that time. Not a John Wayne playing the part of a soldier, but a decorated World War II veteran playing himself on the big screen. He had heard that Audie Murphy once said he was just too afraid not to be a hero. Tom felt that way, too. It wasn't that he wanted to get a medal for bravery, he just needed to know he wasn't a coward. That was the kind of man everyone looked up to, a common man performing uncommon acts of bravery just because it was the right thing to do.

There was also a dark side of the call to arms. A more sinister feeling he did not openly or inwardly admit. Tom Warden wanted to be one of the elite men who could kill without hesitation or remorse. He wanted to be a battle-hardened son of a bitch, one of the hard men who could *pull the trigger*. He wanted his rite of passage. He had chosen the Vietnam War as his battleground to win his manhood. All of that led Tom to seat 16-E on an airplane cruising over the Pacific Ocean on its way to Binh Hua Airfield in South Vietnam just outside of Saigon.

It was a long flight in many ways. There was a feeling of leaving behind and moving toward. A separation of past and future occurred about five hours out of Alaska, after the refueling and crew change. He was aware of where the plane was and where it was headed. He felt somewhat prepared in the sense that Vietnam would be just more military stuff. That relieved some of the unknowns. Like Big Brother would take care of him, bury him if he was killed, bring him home if he was not. The concept of being killed, of dying in combat, was not well formed. Tom Warden was mostly worried about how he would perform as a sergeant and how the seasoned men would accept him. What demands his commanding officer would make. He was not sure if he could kill an enemy soldier. He did not know if he was a coward or not. His gaze and thoughts drifted out through the window toward everything unknown and unprepared for. It was then he felt a fully formed question: *Am I willing to kill a fellow human being so I can have my rite of passage? Yes I am,* was his answer. It happened in an instant. He tried to take it back, to pretend it was different, to pretend it wasn't so. He concealed his choice to kill under a torrent of reason and rhetoric and random thoughts until it was out of conscious thought; then he dozed off.

The change in pitch of the airplane sounds woke him. They were leaving cruising altitude and beginning the final descent. Tom stared out the window, not thinking, just waiting for the first sight of Vietnam. When it came, it was strange and beautiful. They were at about 3,000 feet when the plane crossed the coastline. The sounds of the plane grew louder as it descended more steeply, the *whirrrr* of the flaps extending, the rumble and buffeting, the turbine's lowering pitch. A descending turn brought Tom fully awake.

We're really going to land. Why can't we just turn around and go back? Not enough fuel, not allowed, you made the bargain, what would people think if you quit?

The inevitability of entering a foreign land, a foreign war, loomed over him, pinned him to the present. No exit. No waiting.

The plane went into an incredibly steep descent. Someone said, "They come in steep like this to avoid being shot down." The war had reached up and seized him. He took a deep breath. He felt the busyness of the landing, the pitching, the yawing, the landing gear dropping, the surprise and relief of the touchdown.

The plane taxied toward a huge, hangar-like building. There was a plane already parked there, fuel trucks and baggage carts all around it, and a stairway was being rolled up to it. His plane stopped rolling, the engines spooled down. Tom looked around the cabin. He remembered the old strategy of, *don't be first or last, get somewhere in the middle of the formation to avoid any unexpected special treatment.* The cabin door opened. The light of a foreign sun shone through. The air of a far-off land mixed in and promised to overwhelm the occupants. Tom felt like a giant organism had engulfed the plane and was digesting them.

A spec-4 in jungle fatigues entered the plane and told them they would be filing into a room to the right of the double-door entrance. The passengers began to disembark in an orderly fashion. Tom Warden made an anxious approach to the exit, but had the feeling he was approaching an entrance. He stepped over the threshold on to the top platform of the stairway. The heat hit his face, followed by the odor of jet fuel and damp straw burning.

"Welcome to Nam, suck-a-a-a-s!" One of the soldiers lined up to board the other plane was waving and smiling at the troops on the stairs in front of him. Tom looked into the crowd of men waiting to board the other plane, leave Vietnam, and go back to the world. Most were quiet and intent, focused on the doorway of the waiting plane. A few were jubilant, like the soldier who shouted his welcome. It was the others that held his attention. Their faces at first appeared blank, then one of the somber men offered his eyes to Tom. A presence revealed itself behind that soldier's eyes. Someone was back there in the darkness, looking out past some horizon. That image nullified every idea Tom had about being a soldier and left a void and a promise to fill that void with the reality of war.

"Let's go, Sarge." It was the soldier behind him. For an instant Tom wondered who the guy was talking to. Then Sergeant Warden stepped out and descended the stairway. When his left foot hit the tarmac, it felt like a door slammed behind him. With his next step he made a mental note—*365 days to go*—and joined the men assembled in the converted hangar.

There was a headcount. They were loaded onto buses that would take them to the 90th Replacement Battalion at Long Binh, where they were to go through a six-day orientation and be assigned to a unit. Warden got a window seat on the bus. He was anxious to get a look at this country. Wanted to get a situational awareness. The view from the bus window was like a travel brochure of an exotic Far Eastern land. He tried to imagine that he was on a tour bus taking in the new sites. The feeling didn't last. Sure, there were plenty of Vietnamese on bicycles and three-wheeled Lambretas powered by smoking two-cycle engines. What made the difference was the trucks full of uniformed men with rifles and US army jeeps with mounted machine guns. The most telling scenes were the ARVN soldiers, who were walking on the sidewalk with their weapons slung. They walked, stood, and talked as if they were an everyday part of life. As the bus neared its destination, the view outside the window changed. The number of sandbagged buildings increased. There were chain-link fences topped with concertina wire, then bunkers built of sandbags, then two-story bunkers topped with men standing at machine guns.

The forty-minute tour was over. The bus carrying new troops turned off the paved road and passed between two bunkers. An MP waved them through. Now they were inside a major US base. Here, everyone was in jungle fatigues. Sgt. Warden was surprised to see a few Vietnamese inside the base. All the buildings had a three-foot-high wall of sandbags around them. The buses stopped and a spec-4 herded the FNGs (fucking new guys) to an open area. Tables were set up at the far end of the area. Seated at the tables were the men who kept the army running, the company clerks. They handled all the paperwork. The new troops were divided into alphabetized groups and told to report in file to a specific table.

Sgt. Warden was the first one to walk up to his group's table. The spec-4 did not look up, only asked, "Name, rank, and serial number." That was the moment Sgt. Warden knew he was a prisoner of war. He did not yet realize how long his internment would be.

Blood Sport

Sunday, June 23rd, 1984: Freeland, Indiana

Tom spent the night in in his pickup beside the empty farmhouse. The sun was just showing through the line of trees across the gravel road when he awakened. He wished he could stay there forever and nothing would change. Live by the deserted house and just not wake up some morning. A car pulled into the drive. Tom lit a cigarette and put the .45 caliber automatic lying on the seat into the glove box. When the car came to a stop near his pickup, Tom stepped out and said, "Morning."

The driver of the car smiled as Tom stood. "Hi Tom. Didn't know you were in town."

Tom recognized the man. It was Richard Stoneham. "Hey, Rick. Just got in yesterday for the twentieth reunion."

"Oh yeah, that's right."

"I hear you're on the state police force, Rick."

"Yeah."

"Good for you."

"I was just on my way to the home place when I spotted a strange car. Had to check it out. Force of habit, you know."

"You always had good instincts. Are you going to be here a while?"

"Just today. I'm stationed in Fort Wayne. Gotta be back there tomorrow. What are you doing these days, Tom?"

"Mechanical maintenance at a big health spa. Swimming pool, exercise equipment, all that," Tom lied.

"Sounds like good work."

"Yeah, it's OK. Not much money, though. Last year I had a job keeping books at a nuclear power plant. They made us work six twelve-hour shifts because of the security check. They needed fewer people working a lot of hours. It paid really good, but six twelves a week was more than I could take."

"Yeah, I've done that. Well, I got to go see the folks. Drive safe."

Rick swung the big Buick around and out the drive. The farm fell silent. Tom watched the dust trail kicked up by Rick's car as it sped down the gravel road to his parents' house a mile away. It was opposite the Steiner place. Paul Steiner always had a nice-looking crop of corn. Tom got back in the pickup, cranked it up, drove out the lane past where the garden used to be, and headed to the Walker farm. He and Ted Walker had been buddies in high school and lost touch. It was time to reconnect. He drove past the old fishing hole and turned left toward the Walker farm. *Doesn't seem like twenty years.* Lots of farm homes like this one were still left, but that was changing. Most of the farms had been bought up in two thousand acre enterprises. Ted's dad still farmed the old place where Ted and his dad had both grown up. Tom had a feeling of centuries passing, of almost belonging. The uninterrupted rows of corn in the field across the road, where his great uncle's farmhouse used to be, reminded Tom that he was only visiting.

He turned left into the drive. It felt like he should be on his bicycle meeting his friend to go fishing. It was Sunday and it was summer. Tom spotted a Plymouth Valiant next to the barn. Tom let the pickup roll to a stop by the kitchen door. That was the door they always used. It had a mud room and pantry. Tom smiled when the screen door swung open to reveal Ted standing there, smiling back. He stepped out and approached the truck. Tom got out and they just hugged each other. They held the embrace a moment longer than proper for men of that time.

"You want a beer?" Tom asked.

"Not yet, but I *will* have a J."

"Your mom and dad at church?"

"Yep."

"I'll pull my truck over so they can get through." Tom got back in and drove the pickup onto the lawn. He got out, opened the tailgate, and got a beer from the cooler popping the top as he sat down on the tailgate.

Ted sat next to him and rolled a joint. "You smoke?"

"Not since you came to Indiana University with a cube of hash. That was like fifteen or twenty years ago."

"I was getting some good shit back then. Did you finish at IU?"

"No way. I quit the next day after we smoked that cube. I was miserable, anyway. It wasn't like that first semester at Purdue."

"Yeah, I remember. You used to study all the time."

"That's how I got all those A's."

"Yeah, f'r sure. Let's see. I dropped out and enlisted the winter before. You dropped out and got drafted the next winter. So you must have gone right into IU like a month after you got back from Nam."

"Yep."

"No more A's, huh, Tom?"

"Nope. I couldn't concentrate for more than ten minutes. I struggled through spring semester, then summer school. When you showed up in the middle of the fall semester, I saw the light. Actually, I saw the dark. I never wanted to be a research scientist anyway."

"Bummer." Back in high school we always pictured you as the mad scientist. We got the mad part right. You seem like pissed off at something." Ted held out the joint. "You should have some."

"No thanks, Ted. It just makes me depressed later. A half hour of laughs and half a month of 'Fuck it all'."

"Bummer.

An orange cat appeared from behind the maple tree next to the driveway and sat looking at Tom and Ted. They both watched the cat watching them as Ted spoke. "Whatever happened to you and Shirley? I heard you was engaged."

"Well Ted, she waited till I got back from Nam, then broke off our engagement before I got a chance to. She felt bad. I tried to tell her it was OK, but I don't think it came across. I don't know. Those first few weeks back, I wasn't sure of anything. It felt like I was dropped into the middle of a conversation and everybody was a stranger." The cat got up, and walked away.

Ted looked over at Tom. "Where the hell you living anyway?"

"I moved to Massachusetts a couple years ago."

"Cool weather up there."

"I run numbers and collect the money for some friends in the rackets. Nothing big-time, but they're friends of the family in Providence."

Ted threw his head back, laughed at the sky and said, "You're a gangster! I didn't think you had it in you. Do you carry a piece?"

Tom gave his can of beer a little swirl to check the level. "Sure. I'll show you." He drained his beer and threw the can into the pickup bed. He slid off the tailgate, walked to the passenger side door, opened it, and pulled the .45 caliber automatic from the glove box. As he walked back to the tailgate he, dropped the clip into his left palm and put it in his back pocket. Before he handed the weapon to his friend, he ejected the round from the chamber.

"Always the proper procedure with you, huh, Tom?"

"Can't be too careful."

Ted felt the balance of the weapon and operated the slide. He handed the .45 back to Tom. "I carry a .38 snub-nosed. I can put all five into a five-gallon bucket at fifty feet in five seconds."

"I can believe *that*. Now me, I have to figure if they're fifty feet away, I'd have a better chance of running than shooting a pistol. An M-16 is another story. Nice and long and points easy…real easy." Tom looked at the ground between them.

Ted got up off the tailgate and faced Tom. "You deserved to survive Nam. You know that, don't you?"

"No. No. I don't feel like I should be alive. I should have died there." Tom stepped around to the side of the pickup and retrieved another beer from the cooler. He sat back down on the tailgate and lit a cigarette.

Ted took a final toke and put the roach into a metal snuff can. "I'm working on a second generation roach. When this tin gets full I'm going to roll a mongo joint and smoke it with a bottle of wine." He put the snuffbox in his shirt pocket and buttoned it. "I want to tell you a war story from when I was stationed in Korea. North Korea never signed a peace treaty, you know, just a cease fire agreement."

Ted scooted back into the pickup bed, and leaned against the side. "It was fall, 1968. The North Korean Army had this initiation they made their officers go through. They had them infiltrate the DMZ as their graduation from officer's training school. I was the company clerk, but the executive officer, Lieutenant Bryant, and me would take a Jeep out at night and hunt for the infiltrators. I carried an M-14 with a starlight scope. Once in a while we'd shoot an infiltrator and bring his body back to base. We'd pull into base camp with a North Korean draped over our hood. Just like deer hunting.

"One night we backed the Jeep off the road into some brush and waited. We heard movement and got ready. I was scanning the area with my night scope and saw someone crawling up to the road. The guy started to get up and I whispered, 'Now'. The lieutenant threw on the Jeep headlights and the guy in the road froze in a half crouch. It was an infiltrator. No rifle, just a sidearm. I hesitated. The lieutenant yelled, 'Shoot, for Christ's sakes.' I just held the man in my sights. The lieutenant was yelling 'What the Fuck Ted, what the Fuck?' I lowered my weapon. The infiltrator bolted into the blackness. Me and the lieutenant sat there for about two seconds then he started the Jeep, turned off the lights, and did a one-eighty onto the road. He put some distance between us and where we spotted the infiltrator, then slowed down, stopped the Jeep at the bottom of a grade, and said, 'It's OK, Ted. I understand.' We waited till sunrise to come in so we wouldn't get shot trying to get back on base. The lieutenant never told anyone what happened. I never went out hunting with him again." Ted looked over at Tom.

Tom found his eyes and said, "I wish *I* could have done that one particular night in Nam."

"Yeah? But that's not the end of the story. I was on perimeter guard the night after I let that North Korean infiltrator go. Not in a bunker, but an open firing position on the bunker line. There were four of us in the machine-gun position, but nobody was awake. I'm not sure what woke me, but about three a.m. I opened my eyes and saw a Korean crouching over me. I didn't move, just looked at where his eyes would have been. He touched my throat with the back edge of his knife and jumped out of our foxhole. I drew my .45 and just laid there till morning. I think it was the same North Korean I let go."

Tom took a swallow of beer and lit a cigarette. "They should give you a medal."

"Yeah, they should, but you don't get medals for doing the right thing. You get medals for doing what people want you to do. You get medals for doing what *they* don't want to do or can't bring themselves to do. They give you a medal and hope you stop doing what they gave you the medal for when you get back home. That's the way it is and it's OK with me. I don't care what anybody thinks of me anymore. Well, I care, but not really. What about you, Tom? Do you care what people think?"

Tom flicked cigarette ashes at the ground. "Yes. Yes, I do. I wish I didn't, but I do." He got up and put his weapon back in the glove box.

"Bummer. Sure you don't want some dope?"

"No thanks. I'm going to hang on to what's left of my mind. I haven't got the instincts you have. I don't think I can survive without my mind."

"Yeah? OK, Tom. I still think your head is doing you more harm than good."

Tom allowed a half smile. The two farm boys felt the day shift. It was now late morning and Sunday breakfast would be ready soon. The two combat veterans breathed in the moment, knowing that was all they had.

Ted's mom and dad approached from the west, riding in the same model Ford pickup they always did, just a different year. Gilbert steered the pickup into the lane. The tires never touched the grass growing in the center of the well-defined path. Gil spoke as he stepped from the pickup.

"Good morning, Master Tom."

Jolene walked up to Tom, her purse held in both hands, and stopped before she spoke. "Good to see you, Tom. How are you?"

"I'm pretty good. Came back for the class reunion."

"Got a letter from your mom last week. Said she meets once a month with the ladies from the Arizona Retired Teachers' Association. I guess your dad finished the flagstone patio and is planting shrubbery."

"Yep."

Gil came up and shook Tom's hand. "You staying for breakfast?"

"Sure. That's why I came."

Jolene turned toward the screen door. "Gil got a really good ham from Paul. We'll have some of that."

Gil and Jolene went in. They would change out of their Sunday best. Jolene would start breakfast and Gil would read the Sunday paper. Ted and Tom knew they had some time before breakfast. Ted described how he had built his house in Alabama using the lumber from the old barn on his land. As Ted talked about how well his son was doing in school, Tom was almost frightened by the thought of how different their lives were from what he thought they would be. Tom had been the studious one with a well-ordered future. Ted was the wild one, the prodigal son. Even though Ted lived on the edge of a swamp near the Tensaw River, it was still his place, and he had a son.

As if on cue, Ted and Tom got up and made their way toward the back porch. Maybe it was the scent of biscuits fresh from the oven that drew them, or perhaps the rhythm of farm life had never left them. They entered the kitchen as Ted finished his story about how a water moccasin had chased him in his canoe.

The talk at Sunday breakfast was about gardens and newborns and fences and grain trucks. It could have been 1984 or 1944. This timeless ritual made Tom feel like he was home. He sat with his back to the open porch door, but it did not bother him. He felt nothing could get through there to harm him. The feeling would not last. His unquiet mind called to the world outside and the souls of all the soldiers from all the wars came snuffing across the fields, drawing near. Tom felt like he didn't belong in this holy place. They would find him, the black dogs in his head, and threaten the society of the farm. He had to leave. He would go back to Massachusetts after breakfast. As Tom washed down the last of his ham and eggs with coffee he was thinking. *Long drive back–lots of time to think–Sarah will be waiting*. It was 10:30 Sunday morning.

Honey I'm Home

Wednesday, June 26th, 1984: Fairhaven, Massachusetts

It was dusk when Tom crossed the Rhode Island-Massachusetts border. He had driven straight through from Indiana, but he felt almost refreshed. Over the years he had learned how to make good time on the road without getting burned out. He felt more at ease on the open road than anywhere else. By the time he pulled into Sarah's driveway, he was already reorienting himself to the present. There was money to collect, a new guy to break in, the remodel job at the bar Sarah had just purchased. Tom had called from Pennsylvania and told her when he would be home, but she wasn't there to meet him. *Probably at the new bar*. His tools were there, too. He would resume work in the morning. He could get a day's work done before he collected the numbers and cash from the bookies tomorrow night.

They had been living together for over a year, but Sarah's house on West Island did not feel like home. It was her house. Tom had never owned a house. Never had a job long enough to establish credit. Sarah allowed for Tom's "week off" once in a while. She understood. Sarah needed some time to herself now and then anyway. Just like tonight. It wasn't that she didn't love Tom, she just didn't need him. Sarah and Tom had moved in together a couple of weeks after they met. The job he followed to Massachusetts was almost over, so he quit and went to work for Sarah's friend, Finger, a small-time racketeer.

Tom got his bag from the pickup bed, went to the door, and let himself in. He unpacked his bag mostly into the washer and added detergent. Sarah liked things neat. Tom did, too, but didn't always think it was worth the trouble to keep up. The kitchen, laundry, and family room were in the same space. He opened the yellow fridge and got the makings for a ham sandwich. *Sarah must be at the bar*, he thought again. He wanted to go find her, but knew better.

He flipped on the television, and changed to the news channel, *Nothing major going on. No war anyway*. Moscow's boycott of the Summer Olympics in Los Angeles was getting plenty of coverage. Sarah had been following Mary Lou Retton and the rest of America's women's gymnastic team since 1981. Sarah was obsessed with the Olympics. The gymnastic events were her favorite. They wouldn't start until the end of July, but Tom thought she would still be home in time to watch the eleven o'clock sports coverage. The USSR had announced its intention not to participate in the Olympics last month, so even the news channels were covering the Olympics.

Sarah had played tennis from grade school through college. She had been a fierce competitor on the amateur tennis tour for five years. At one time she had dreams of playing professionally, but injuries and alcohol ended them. Only the best of the best got there. Sarah didn't think she was the best, even when she was. That was hard on her. She wanted to win the gold in everything she did. When she won first place in a local tennis tournament, she was elated for a day or two, then it was back to training so she could win again. When she came in second, she felt worthless. There was no in-between.

About 11:30, Tom heard a car in the drive. He got up and went directly to the door and opened it just as Sarah was fishing for her keys. Tom smiled and said, “Hi.”

“Oh! I didn’t think you’d still be up.”

Tom’s smile dropped as he stepped aside so Sarah could come in. She placed her purse on the counter and turned to greet Tom. She extended her arms and placed her palms on his shoulders.

“So, how was your trip?”

“Not what I expected. Not at all really.”

“What did you expect?” She gripped Tom’s shoulders and nudged him closer, then let her hands slip down his arms.

“I expected to sit and talk about old times, but it was the same talk about *these* old times. Not much changed but the size of the farms.”

“Did they think you had changed?”

“Yeah, I think they did. They didn’t think I did some of the things I’ve done since I saw them last. I didn’t tell them I worked for a gangster, though.”

“You mean me? I’m not a gangster.” She started to smile.

Tom pulled her closer. “So how about some pasta?” That was not what Tom wanted, but some pasta might help. Sarah was slow to warm up. She slipped around the end of the counter and removed a pot from the bottom cupboard.

"Get some of Mom's meatballs from the freezer," she said over her shoulder. He got the meatballs and put them in the saucepan that she had put on the burner. Sarah got the salad bowl and the cutting board. Tom passed a tomato, a cucumber, and a head of lettuce out of the fridge. Sarah relayed the vegetables to the counter next to the chopping block. She began to slice and dice. He peeled a couple cloves of garlic and mashed them with salt in a mortar. She halved a lemon and squeezed it into the salt and garlic, pressing her breasts against his arm as she moved. Sarah glanced back at him as she went to stir the sauce and meatballs. Tom sliced bread and spread garlic butter. The kitchen was starting to smell good.

When she bent down to get bowls for the spaghetti. Tom said, "Those jeans fit nice."

Sarah smiled. "And don't you forget it."

"I never do."

Sarah dropped some spaghetti into the boiling water. "You should put your bread in the oven, Tom."

"Do you think the oven's hot enough?"

"You'll have to see won't you?" Tom bent down and got a pan from the lower cabinet. "Those jeans fit nice," she said. Tom smiled. "Any of your old girlfriends like your jeans?"

"No comments from the old flames," he said as he turned toward her. "Why do you worry about that? Even if I was looking, which I'm not, I don't want to be with anyone but you."

"Yeah, yeah, sure. Check the spaghetti."

There was a bottle of wine on the counter. He opened it and poured them each a glass. Tom never drank wine unless Sarah did. They sat on bar stools at the counter and ate the salad. After the spaghetti and meatballs, they cleaned up and washed the dishes in silence.

When Sarah finished wiping down the counter, she tossed the sponge into the sink and looked at Tom. He wiped his hands on the dishtowel and placed it next to Sarah. She leaned back against the counter. Tom leaned in. She raised her face toward him.

He kissed her on her forehead, her lips, her neck, her shoulders. His hands found the small of her back. He kissed her breasts, her hands, then her belly, and stayed there for a while. His hands traced down her thighs behind her knees. When Tom felt a slight tremor he picked her up and carried her to the bedroom. He liked undressing Sarah. It was nice and she let him. He took his time because he knew when the lovemaking was over she wouldn't want to be touched.

He was so in love with Sarah. He felt it most when they made love, but it was the only time Sarah seemed to be in love with him. The rest of the time she was just his friend. He tried to stay awake. Most of the time he could, but not tonight. The road had been too long. Before he dozed off, he said, "I love you, Sarah, I love you."

His breathing became heavy. Sarah brushed the hair back from his forehead and said, "I love you too, Tom, and don't you forget it."

Tom was asleep when the alarm went off. Sarah was in the shower, so Tom went to the kitchen and made coffee. He was staring at the countertop with a bagel in his hand when Sarah looked around the fridge and said, “Two bagels would be nice.”

“OK…I’ll see what I can do.” He set the bagel on a plate and followed her down the hall. She turned right into the bedroom and closed the door. He went straight into the bathroom and took a shower.

Tom focused on what he needed to do today. It gave him some relief from the turmoil in his mind. Sarah had purchased a neighborhood bar, the Blue Oyster, in the town of Fairhaven across the harbor from New Bedford. It was a fishermen’s bar and could get rowdy sometimes. None of the captains allowed liquor on their trawlers. The trips out to George’s Banks would last seven to ten days. It was grueling and dangerous work, and at the end of the trip the Blue Oyster was one of the places the fishermen came to unwind. The place needed a lot of work to bring it up to building and health codes. Sarah had asked him to do the work and Tom had readily agreed. It wasn’t his favorite kind of work, but he liked working for and with Sarah.

“Back to work,” he said to the showerhead as he shut off the water. His mind wandered. *The honeymoon is over. This isn’t going to work. Who am I kidding?* Sarah loved him as much as she could but couldn’t get any closer. Neither could Tom. He couldn’t tell her everything. He hadn’t ever cheated on her, but it felt like he had. He had talked about things with Murphy and Ted that he would never talk about with her. He trusted Sarah, but his balance—his sense of worth—depended on her too much to risk telling her anything that might change the way she felt about him. Maybe that's why she didn't trust him. Maybe she knew there was something he wasn't telling.

Sarah was eating a bagel with cream cheese when Tom came into the kitchen pulling a T-shirt over his head. "You can have the other half. I'm going to the Blue Oyster. You coming?"

"Yes, I'm coming. You know I'm coming. I said I was coming to help you. I'll come in my truck so I can haul lumber."

"Just checking in, Tom. You change your mind sometimes."

"I haven't changed my mind about anything."

Sarah slung her bag over her shoulder, went to the front door, and looked back. "OK…and remember you have to pick up money from Bobby tonight." Sarah made her exit with her usual stride.

The money Tom would pick up from Bobby came from the numbers racket, Sarah's side business with Finger. It was like the Massachusetts state lottery, but winning bets were paid off in cash, so they were tax-free. The business was not immoral, but it was illegal.

Bobby was one of Finger's bookies. He took bets from the locals and held the money, some of which he would use to pay off customers who "hit" their number. At the end of a week, there was always money left over (never bet against the house). Whenever there was a big hit, Finger had to call "the bank"—that was Sarah—and get some extra money for the payoff. That didn't happen too often.

Along with the banker and the bookies there was the bagman—that was Tom. He collected from the bookies weekly and when there was a big hit he would take the cash to the bookie to cover the payoff. The numbers the customers would bet on were the last three digits of the day's trading volume on the New York Stock Exchange. You could also find the winning number the next morning in the *Providence Journal* or *Boston Globe*. If betting on one particular number was too heavy, Sarah would call one of two other "bankers" in town and lay off some of the bets on that number. Local law enforcement didn't bother any of the bankers or bookies. They liked to play the tax-free numbers, too. Besides, it was all local and nobody got hurt.

Tom arrived at the Blue Oyster just after Sarah. They had planned the layout weeks ago, so he went right to work without talking to her. She was in and out all day, so they spoke very little. She was gone when he finished his day's work. Tom felt it was a good day. He cleaned up the job site and headed for the Ferry Café to make his first money pick-up. The Ferry Café was a bar at night, a café in the daytime, and always a place where you could place a bet on the daily number. It was about 6:30 p.m. when Tom arrived and sat down in the corner booth by the swinging doors, which led to the kitchen.

Bobby came over and said, "How ya doing, Shrub?"

That's what the boys called Tom, The Shrub.

"I'm doing OK."

"You have a nice vacation?"

"Yeah, nice."

Bobby looked out at the street. "Kentucky, was it?"

"Indiana. A class reunion in Indiana. What happened at Ivy Street?"

"Drug bust."

"No way."

"Yeah. That's where the money is these days." Bobby leaned in and lowered his voice. "Finger don't want any part of it, but maybe he has no choice."

"Well," Tom said, "this is a quiet neighborhood. Maybe we can keep it that way."

"Sure, Shrub."

The bartender came around the bar with a brown paper bag and a coffee to go.

"Here's your baklava."

"Thanks, man." Tom set the brown bag beside him in the booth and took the lid off the coffee. As he reached into the bag for a wedge of baklava, he checked for the cash under it, then looked at Bobby. "OK."

Bobby held Tom's eyes. "Say Shrub, you want to leave your piece here?"

"Not really. Should I?"

"Yeah, I think so. The cops are searching any unsavory individuals, such as yourself, and questioning them. If you was to have a deadly weapon, it would upset them."

Tom shrugged and said, "What if somebody tries to rob me?"

"Hey, no need to kill anybody over money. Finger don't want that."

"OK." Tom went to his pickup and returned with a small toolbox. He set it on the floor and slid back into the booth.

Bobby retrieved a folded paper from his pocket and handed it to Tom. It was a deposit ticket. "It matches what's there," Bobby said, nodding toward the bag beside Tom. "Just in case you need to explain why you happen to have a few grand cash in your possession."

Tom leaned over, opened his toolbox and put the deposit ticket in the top tray. Then he lifted the tray enough for Bobby to see the gun, and put the brown bag under the tray.

"The Roach will show you what needs to be fixed," Bobby said as he got up and went to the register to ring up a customer. Tom slid out of the booth with his toolbox and pushed through the doors back into the kitchen.

The Roach was stirring a cauldron of clam chowder. Ashes dropped from his cigarette into the steaming liquid as he bent to check if it had the proper fragrance. The man stirring the clam chowder was Leonard Roche. His older brother was a detective with the Fairhaven Police Department. Tom swung the toolbox onto the stainless steel counter beside the stove and said, "Hey Roach, Bobby said you had a screw loose."

"Yeah? He's the one with a loose screw." The Roach looked down at Tom's toolbox. "You got a tool you won't be needing?" Tom nodded. Leonard, The Roach, motioned Tom to follow him to a corner of the kitchen where he had an office set up. In general, the kitchen was clean, but chaotic. The office area was different. The desktop was clear except for a To-Do list. There were three letter trays on the shelf above the desk labeled Mail, Bills, and File. The mail and file trays were empty. The tray for bills contained three or four neatly stacked invoices. Tom set his toolbox on the floor and retrieved the .45 automatic from his toolbox, handing it to Roach. Leonard released the magazine, operated the side to make sure there was no round in the chamber. He aimed at the desk, and dropped the hammer. He snapped the magazine back into the butt, then locked the weapon in the side drawer of his desk.

"You can come get it when you're not working. OK?"

"OK." Tom picked up his toolbox. He felt uneasy, cautious. It wasn't about giving up his weapon. There was something about his surroundings that put him on alert. Anything that didn't feel normal stirred a primal fear in him. He looked around the kitchen, then back at The Roach. "I don't see any recipe books. Don't you need recipes?"

"I joined the Navy when I was seventeen. They made me a cook. I memorized all the recipes. It made life simpler. Habits you learn when you're a young man die hard. I've memorized a lot of recipes over the years." The Roach tilted his head slightly forward and looked at Tom. Tom shifted his toolbox to his left hand and walked out of the kitchen.

On his way back to the truck, he scanned the sidewalk and parking lot for new faces or anything out of place. As he approached his truck, a man's voice came from behind.

"Hey, Tom..." Tom dropped his toolbox and jumped between his pickup and the car parked next to it. "You forgot your coffee." It was Bobby.

"Oh...thanks."

"You OK, Shrub?"

"Yeah, yeah. No sweat." Tom accepted the coffee from Bobby, picked up his toolbox, and got in his truck. As he drove out of the parking lot he was thinking, *The Roach was right, habits you learn when you're a young man die hard.*

Life and Death

Friday, June 28th, 1984: Fairhaven, Massachusetts

Timmy Furtado was short and skinny with the fingers of an artist. He always wore nice slacks, dress shoes, and an Eisenhower jacket. Timmy kept books for one of the ship chandleries on Union Street. He was picked up for drunk driving last winter and lost his driver's license. Timmy also sold cocaine on the waterfront. Some of the fishermen used coke to get through the long hours out on the trawlers. Timmy was not big-time, just a few regular customers. Timmy Furtado left the Sand Dollar bar at 7:30 p.m. He bought a quart of Budweiser, and then walked towards Cottage Street where he lived on the top floor of a two decker.

Timmy climbed the side stairs and was fumbling with his set of keys when the door opened. He jumped back. His back hit the railing and he started to go over backwards. The man in the doorway was quick and sure. He grabbed for Timmy's flailing right arm and pulled him back on to the second-story landing.

"Let me take that for you, Timmy," he said as he took hold of the quart bottle that was still clutched in Tim's left hand.

Timmy held on to the beer and allowed himself to be led into the apartment by the man. The man released the bottle and closed the door. Timmy set the quart of beer on the kitchen counter. The porch light next door was all that shined through the kitchen window.

Timmy tried to speak, "You…you…you."

A second man stepped up behind Timmy and trapped him with a bear hug. The first man slapped Timmy across the face with a meaty hand. The second man forced Timmy to his knees and held him there, bearing down on his shoulders. The first man dragged a chair from the table and pushed the back against Tim's chest, then straddled the chair.

"You owe money. You owe more money than you got." He put a hand on top of Tim's head and rocked it from side to side. "Isn't that so, Tim?"

"I can get it."

"Don't lie to me, Tim. It's a sin to lie, and sins are punished."

"No, really. I can." The man behind Timmy rapped Timmy's ear with his knuckles. "God damn it, that hurts."

The man in front seized a handful of Timmy's hair and jerked it back. "Don't take the name of the Lord in vain, Tim."

"S-s-sorry."

"What about the money, Timmy?"

"How much time have I got?"

"Oh Timmy, you're out of time. We might come for you in the morning, or maybe next week. You need to be ready when we come."

The man in front pulled an ice pick from his back pocket and laid the tip inside Timmy's nostril. Timmy was looking cross-eyed at the utensil when the man in back put him in a headlock. The man in front slid the device a little farther in.

"If you don't have an offering when we come back, I will probe deeper. Deep enough to find out what's on your mind."

The man in back chuckled. The man with the ice pick sprang back with the chair. The man in back shoved Timmy's face down, drove a knee into his back, and released him. Timmy crawled under the kitchen table.

"N-n-no, please no, God, no." He crawled out the other side and rolled his back against the wall, arms up to protect himself. The room was empty, the door closed. Timmy crawled out of the kitchen through the living room and into his bedroom. He walked his hands up the wall and stumbled to the closet. He reached under a pile of clothes on the top shelf and pulled out a .45 automatic, Army issue. He sank down in the closet and pulled the door closed behind him.

It was nine o'clock when Timmy thought of a way out. He had bet on the daily number enough and knew one of the bagmen. He knew the money pick-up would be later that night behind Kruger's antique shop.

"Thursday night, right? Yes, that's right," Timmy said aloud. He crawled out of the closet, stood, and hung up his jacket. He took a step back, scanning the room. He went to the chest of drawers and pulled on the top drawer. It tilted toward him. "What the Fuck." He lost his grip on the .45. "Fuck! Fucking drawers." Timmy unstuck the dresser drawer, found his blackjack, picked up the pistol, and set it on top of the chest of drawers. Timmy turned on the lamp and looked at the clock. He went into the closet, and grabbed a hooded sweatshirt. He pulled it on, and slid the .45 under his belt in the small of his back and put the blackjack in the front pouch of the sweatshirt.

Timmy always got someone else to drive his car, but tonight he'd have to chance driving without a license. He drove the mile to the antique shop. At 9:10 he backed his car into a space near the back and waited. At 9:30, the bagman came from the side parking lot, headed for the back door. Timmy knew the bagman's routine. One of Timmy's customers lived across the alley behind the shop and he had seen the bagman use the back door several times.

Timmy looked over the whole parking lot. Before he got out of his car, he took the bulb out of the dome light. There was a dumpster near the back door of the antique shop, so he sat against the wall in its shadow. Within ten minutes, the back door of the antique shop swung open. Hack, the bagman, stepped out and waited for the steel door to close, then pushed and pulled the door handle to make sure it was locked.

Timmy took an overhand swing at the bagman's head just as he was turning. The blackjack clipped the side of Hack's head then continued on, cracking his collarbone. Hack dropped the bag of money then raised his good arm in front of his face. Timmy swung at it then began wild blows as fast as he could swing the blackjack. The bagman went down. He fell back against the block wall and pulled his knees up. Timmy kept swinging. Hack rolled over and tried to crawl away.

Timmy landed a blow to the back of the bagman's head. Hack slumped unconscious. Timmy snatched the brown bag off the ground and started to run around the end of the building then held up and walked with his head down to his car. He drove half a block, pulled into a parking lot, then checked for the blackjack and gun.

"OK, OK." He reached into the brown bag and pulled out the cash and counted the bills, thirteen one-hundred-dollar bills and two twenties. "Fuck!" Timmy needed five thousand dollars.

He pulled the car back onto the street, heading away from where he lived. He drove randomly for a while and ended up on a country road. He drove about ten miles, then turned around and went back to New Bedford. When he got back into town, Timmy drove past his place on Cottage Street, scanning the street and narrow driveways between the two-deckers. He drove around the block and continued on to a pool hall on Purchase Street he'd been in once or twice. He waited for a man to pass on the sidewalk and pulled into the parking lot. He got out of the car and felt the .45 slipping sideways in his belt, so he pulled it out and put it under the seat. He started to close the door, then turned and tossed the blackjack onto the back seat. He locked the car. After taking a deep breath, he stepped off toward the pool hall.

The man on the sidewalk watched Timmy saunter to the pool hall entrance. When Timmy entered the pool hall, the man approached Timmy's car and tried the driver's door. It was locked. He tried the passenger door. It was not. He looked around the parking lot then slid onto the seat, pulling the door closed without slamming it. He looked at the dome light and saw there was no cover and no bulb. He continued his motion and reached under the seat with a gloved hand and found the weapon. He peered out the driver's side window, his body stretched out across the front seat. With one motion he rolled over the seatback into the backseat face up. He waited and listened.

In the pool hall, Timmy was finishing off a beer. He paid with one of the twenties from the bag, dropped a tip on the counter, and headed for the door. He stopped at a cigarette machine and looked at all the brands, then left the pool hall.

The man in the backseat heard someone approaching and slid onto the floor. Timmy unlocked the car door and got in. He jiggled the key into the ignition, started the engine and threw his right arm over the back seat.

The man in the backseat sat up behind him.

"Busy night?"

Timmy recoiled into the steering wheel. "Oh Jesus, Fuck—Shit! I didn't mean to swear. I swear to God I didn't. I've got some of the money."

"I don't want your money and I don't mind if you swear."

"You don't? But…what? You're not them…him?"

The man in the backseat laid the barrel of the .45 over the seat pointing it at Timmy's heart. "Not him? Not who?"

"The guy with the ice pick."

"Oh. Sounds like an interesting fellow. I'd like to meet him."

"No, no, you don't want to meet him."

"Sounds like you don't want to meet him again, either."

"I wish I'd never met him."

"Oh?"

"Who the hell are you, anyway?"

"That's not important."

"It's important to me because you're the guy in my backseat pointing a gun at my chest. Hey, is that my gun?"

"It was under your seat, so I suppose it is."

Timmy turned his back closer to the car door.

"Why don't you stay a while and talk? Maybe I can help you, mister…?"

"Timmy. Call me Timmy. Who *are* you?"

"I am the guy in your backseat with a gun, so I get to ask the questions. You get to answer."

"OK?"

"Put your seatbelt on, Timmy." Timmy faced the front and slumped back. "Your seatbelt, please." The man tapped Timmy's shoulder with the .45 muzzle. Timmy looked in the rearview mirror and fastened his seatbelt. "Let's go to Fort Phoenix Beach where we can see the harbor."

Timmy started the car and backed out. They drove to the Fort Phoenix Beach state reservation at the south end of Fairhaven and parked where a maple tree sheltered them from a street light. Timmy shut the engine off.

The man in the backseat said, "Hand me the keys." Timmy held the keys over his shoulder. A gloved hand took them.

"Do you like to watch the boats, Timmy?"

"I hate boats. I get sick. People drown."

"I like to watch boats. I like to imagine they're always coming and going to some exotic place."

"What's this all about? You said you could help."

"I was wondering if you ever killed anyone, Timmy."

"What?"

"Did you ever kill anybody?"

"No."

"Do you think you could, Timmy, if you were scared enough?"

"Maybe. How about you mister? You ever kill anybody?"

The man in the backseat said, "Yes. Yes I have."

Timmy swallowed hard and looked in the rearview mirror. "You said you could help? You want me to kill somebody for money?"

"No, Timmy."

"OK, then what?"

"I'm going to kill you, Timmy."

Timmy jerked forward and sucked in air. "What? You're…why? Why you gonna kill me?"

"I like killing people."

"Well, kill somebody else!"

The man settled back, and sighed. "What's your biggest regret Timmy?"

"Getting in the car with you."

"Now, now, Timmy, don't be funny. This is serious."

"No shit."

"Go ahead, tell me. What's your biggest regret?"

"Well, ahh, my, uhm…not doing it with one of the cheerleaders back in high school."

"Really?"

"Yeah. I think about that. I think I could've done anything I wanted after that."

"That would have changed your life?"

"Yeah. I think it would."

"Do you have any family, Tim?"

"No. Mom died six years ago. My dad died on a fishing boat. Got knocked overboard. That was a long time ago."

"Are you afraid, Tim?"

"I was a minute ago." Tim turned to look at the man in the back. "Maybe it wouldn't be such a bad thing…dying, I mean. I'm a coke addict and there are two guys looking for me who are going to shove an ice pick up my nose if I don't give 'em five grand." Timmy looked out the passenger side window. "You really gonna kill me?"

"Yes, I am."

Timmy blinked back tears. "I was thinking maybe if I lived a little while longer, I could find that cheerleader."

"Do you really think that would happen?"

"Nah. I guess not." Timmy leaned back against the driver's side door, and placed his leg up on the seat. "I feel sick."

"That's normal. Tell me, Tim, do you want to say goodbye to anyone, leave them a message?"

"Well…no. Nobody." Tim faced the windshield, and held his head in both hands. "Am I hearing this right mister? You've done this before. You kill people because you like it?"

"Yes, that's right."

"Holy Fuck, and I was afraid to ask that cheerleader for a date."

"Ahh, you see my point, then. If you can kill somebody, just...because it feels good, you can do anything after that."

"Wow." Timmy leaned back in the seat and slapped the steering wheel. "Wow!"

The man in the backseat placed the muzzle of the .45 close to Tim's skull.

"The problem is, Tim, when you kill someone for the pleasure of it, you *could* do anything else, but you don't *want* to do anything else."

The .45 slug went into the back of Timmy's head at 900 feet per second and left his forehead, along with all his hopes and dreams. It was midnight.

Unmarked Grave

March 1969: Republic of South Vietnam

The sun was about to rise. Alpha Company was getting ready for a three-day operation along the Van Co Dong River, not far from the Cambodian border. They were loaded with extra ammo and water because it was going to be a slumber party. They would go out this morning on choppers to the Plain of Reeds north of the Cu Chi tunnels. Patrols had spotted VC and NVA activity in that specific area, so Alpha Company anticipated a hot LZ.

Tom adjusted the new issue gas mask on his rucksack. He really liked it; only about one-third the weight of the old one and in a waterproof pouch, too. They were using a rice paddy just outside the firebase as an assembly area. They humped out of the firebase between two bunkers on either side of the main gate down to the road that led to a village. About two hundred yards outside the wire, the men began lining up, forming six- and seven-man groups staggered out across the rice paddy. Sgt. Warden split his squad into two groups about fifteen yards apart and he took his place on a line between them, a little upwind of where their chopper would land, and dropped his rucksack. Phil the machine gunner, Villalobos M-16, and Jefferson M-79 grenade launcher—all seasoned troops, were in one group. They would load up on the left side of the chopper. Sgt. Warden, Woody (Warden's RTO), and Rawlings, the FNG, would load up on the right side of the chopper.

Rawlings had been in country about a month. This was his second chopper ride. Warden always kept the green troops close to him. Rawlings was walking point today. The reality was that all six of them would be on point the first few minutes when they hit the LZ and fanned out toward the brush line.

Sgt. Warden could hear the choppers now. *The LZ will be hot.* He felt the undercurrent of fear surface. He automatically detached from the reality of what was happening. The CO popped smoke. Tom got up, slung on his rucksack, and faced the flight of choppers. The lead ship swept over Warden. He counted and picked out the chopper that would pick his squad up.

Like dancers, the choppers performed a simultaneous flare. The maneuver slowed their descent and forward motion. It looked like they were digging their heels into the ground. The rotor blades bit hard, making the *whop whop whop* louder and louder.

Sgt. Warden raised his M-16 over his head with both hands, his eyes locked on his bird. The turbine whine was louder. The bird for first squad thundered over him and Sgt. Warden bent his knees slightly and brought the M-16 a little forward and down as he tried to lock eyes with the pilot. Warden lowered his M-16 to a point where he could see the nose of the chopper over the line of the weapon. As the ship got closer and lower, Warden brought the M-16 lower and lower until his line of sight over the weapon lined up with the chopper's landing skids. Just before the bird was over the spot between his men, Warden dropped to one knee and lowered his M-16 to the ground, as if he were giving homage to a god.

The pilot set the bird down between Warden's men like it was the only thing he had ever done or would ever do. His men moved toward the chopper and pulled themselves in. Warden hustled in an arc around the rotor blades, which were already tilting forward and lower out in front in preparation for takeoff. The new guy jumped his attention from one place to another at random. Sgt. Warden boosted himself onto the floor of the chopper and wrapped his left arm around the leg of the copilot's seat. Woody sat on the floor behind him. Four men sat on a bench facing forward: Rawlings, on the right, then Jefferson, and Phil next with his M-60 between his legs, the butt resting on the floor. Next to him was Villalobos. Sgt. Warden sat on the edge of the floor with his feet hanging out the doorway. He could see the terrain better like that. If he leaned out a little, he could even see the terrain ahead.

The pilot pulled back on the collective and the rotor blades pulled the war machine up and forward. The sound was heavier and deeper with the added weight of Sgt. Warden's men and their gear. Warden felt a little rush as they became airborne. He knew to keep the adrenaline to a minimum at the start of a mission. No use getting worked up over something that *might* happen. He allowed himself the excitement of the ascent into safety. At about fifty feet the door gunner looked around at Rawlings who was leaning forward trying to see out the door. The gunner shook Rawlings' knee and said something Warden couldn't hear. Rawlings smiled and nodded. The door gunner settled back and closed his eyes. At 200 feet the flight of thirteen slicks turned west toward Cambodia. Their flight path would take them over the northern part of the Mekong Delta into the Plain of Reeds. It wasn't often Warden allowed himself a break. There was nothing he could do for the next 30 minutes. He had formed a mental picture of the LZ, while marking possible artillery targets on his waterproof map along with their coded coordinates. It was just a precaution. He wouldn't need to direct artillery unless the CO and a few lieutenants got hit. There was no need to be poised for action at this moment. He would let the pilot be responsible for his fate and the fate of his men. Anyway, it was safe up here. No reminders of home, of what he would miss if he died, or what he couldn't do if he lost a limb. He had been in country a long time now and whenever he was up in the choppers, he had the feeling of not wanting to descend, wanting to stay in this make-believe world forever.

Tom Warden watched the ground as they passed over the green of the delta. South Vietnam was beautiful from the air. He didn't think of the land below as being South Vietnam. He was aware of the beauty he was passing over. He let his mind go. Let time go. He could see the dots of water buffalo in the green of marsh and paddies. He was not thinking of past or present. The land below seemed separated from war. From above, there was no presence of war in the land. There were no bomb craters this close to Saigon. No thoughts of battle. Tom let himself be lulled by the slowly passing green of a tropical paradise.

In fifteen minutes he was drawn from his sanctuary. The whining of the turbines was different. Tom felt the choppers tilt forward and down, beginning their descent. The rotor sounds softened. Sgt. Warden released his fantasy of peace and wrapped his arm tighter around the leg of the copilot's seat before he leaned out and looked ahead, *Five or six minutes to the LZ.* Sgt. Warden craned his neck and checked his squad. Woody was asleep. Villalobos was scanning the terrain on the left. Phil locked the bolt back on his M-60. He wouldn't set a belt of ammo in until he was on the ground. Rawlings tapped a twenty-round magazine on his knee and locked it into his weapon. Jefferson stopped chewing gum long enough to smile at his sergeant. Whenever Warden asked Jefferson why he was smiling, Jefferson would say, "*We're still alive, ain't we*?" So Warden knew what the smile meant. The door gunner unstrapped his M-60 and swung it into firing position.

They were at five hundred feet. Warden leaned out and scanned ahead. He saw a Huey gunship passing out front, making a pass at the LZ. He could see the tracers. At two hundred feet, Warden spotted a single VC running away from the LZ. The chopper rocked back on its heels, the rotor blades digging into the air, bleeding off airspeed and altitude fast. At fifty feet, the door gunner opened fire. Warden uncradled his weapon and chambered a round, then edged out a little farther. Woody got in a kneeling position behind Warden. Ten feet. The door gunner stopped firing. Five feet. The choppers would not touch down, or even stop and hover. Two feet. Warden shoved out onto the landing skid, then jumped to the ground in one motion and kept moving for another ten yards in a crouch. He looked back and saw Woody and Rawlings coming toward him. The chopper was already past and gaining altitude, rotor blades popping. The door gunner opened up again. It was hard to hear the pop and crack of incoming small arms fire at that point, unless it was really close, and it was really close. When the choppers got a little higher Sgt. Warden could hear the rattle of another AK off in the direction the choppers were leaving. *Probably shooting at the slicks*. Villalobos was taking his fire team to Warden's right, linking up with third squad. Warden moved out with his team and linked up with first squad on his left. As the squads linked up, Lieutenant Stark was signaling them to move out to the perimeter of the LZ. First platoon was on the other side of the LZ, and the two platoons started to close the gap toward the front of the LZ.

The two platoons had barely moved twenty yards into the brush and started cover fire when the third platoon and the CO jumped off the second flight of choppers in the LZ. In less than five minutes, Alpha Company had landed and formed a perimeter. In another five minutes the rifle company was moving in three columns in the direction that the running VC was spotted. Warden's squad had point for second platoon. Sgt. Warden had Rawlings on point. Warden walked second, with Woody third, then Phil with the M-60, and Jefferson next. Villalobos was a short-timer. He walked last and watched everyone so they didn't screw up and get him killed. When they had moved about fifty yards into the brush, Warden looked back to check the spacing and just see how everyone was doing. Jefferson saw Warden looking at him and grinned. *Right, we're still alive.*

The men of Alpha Company settled into a steady rhythm. They were humping the bush, looking for weapons caches and hoping that VC didn't round up some friends and set up an ambush. Warden had a feeling that wouldn't happen. The VC were not a bunch of renegades. If their mission was to bring weapons and supplies in close to Saigon, that's what they would do without any contact with GIs. Still, if the company was not on a specific infiltration route the local VC used someone was likely to get blown up by a booby trap.

By mid-afternoon Alpha Company was searching an area of abandoned rice paddies and overgrown dikes. All civilians in the area were relocated years ago. This was now a free fire zone. That meant more than the men of Alpha Company were free to fire at anyone out here. They were *required* to fire at anyone out here. It was understood that their mission, official or not, was to get a body count.

Warden heard someone break squelch twice on the radio, then the voice of the lieutenant's RTO announced, "Find some shade and take ten. Then we got to search the dikes."

Woody unclipped the handset and answered, "Roger that Oscar Two." RTOs in the same company recognized each others' voices, so rarely used their official call signs. The other two squad RTOs gave their *roger thats*.

Sgt. Warden approached the nearest dike coming up behind his point man. They moved along the dike in opposite directions, checking for trip wires and any disturbed ground that indicated a buried weapons cache. The rest of the squads spread out along the dike and made their own check before sitting down in the shade provided by the brush and nipa palm growing on it. This dike was about three feet high and four feet wide. The brush partially obscured his view of first platoon on the next dike thirty yards away. Warden put one knee on the dike, then turned and sat back on the rounded edge.

When he set the butt of his rifle beside him, it felt softer than it should have. He bumped the surface again with the butt of his rifle, harder this time. It sounded hollow. Warden fixed his bayonet and started to probe. He found bamboo slats covered with cloth under about two or three inches of dirt and leaves. The slats formed a cover for a hidden trench containing three 155 mm rockets. Villalobos found part of what appeared to be a large plank of wood farther down the dike. Rawlings helped Villalobos dig away the 6 inches of dirt covering it while Sgt. Warden set up a charge of C-4 on the 155 mm high explosive rockets.

Before he finished, Rawlings said, "Hey, Sarge."

"What?"

"It's a coffin."

"Well, open it."

"I ain't gonna open a fucking coffin."

"You never seen a dead body?"

"It's somebody's grave, man."

Sgt. Warden stepped back from his demolition work and started toward Rawlings and the coffin. "I'll do it. The rest of you clear out and get behind that dike." He pointed to another dike that intersected the one where they had found the weapons cache and coffin.

He went up to the coffin and jammed his bayonet under the lid and pried. It loosened and left a gap large enough to get his fingers under. With his left palm on the ground, he grabbed the coffin lid, and heaved. The lid gave way a lot easier than he expected and he sprawled across the coffin, his face inches from the brown grin of the corpse inside. He shoved himself back and onto his feet. Warden had the distinct impression the corpse opened its eyes in surprise and protest at being disturbed by the living. He took a breath and inched back toward the remains. He looked at the eyes to make sure they were closed.

"Sarge."

Warden spun around. "Fuck! Jesus, Woody, why are you still here?"

"LT says blow the cache and move out. First platoon captured a VC hiding in a spider hole. We got to secure an LZ so as a chopper can pick'im up."

Warden turned and flipped the coffin lid back, not quite getting it closed.

"We going to cover it back up, Sarge?"

"No."

"We should cover it back up, Sarge."

"I know, Woody, I know. There's no time. Get behind the fucking dike with the rest of the squad."

Woody looked over at the unearthed grave, then walked toward the dike and joined the rest of the squad behind it.

Sgt. Warden lit the one-minute fuse. “Fire in the hole! Fire in the hole!”

He strode off and took cover behind the dike with his squad. Fifteen seconds later, the explosion put a nice gap in the dike where the enemy rockets had been stashed. After the prisoner was picked up, Alpha Company dug in for the night. At o-three-hundred hours, Sgt. Warden was awake on his watch, looking back toward the way they had come, half expecting the unquiet dead to come for him out of the mist. He knew the rats had found the corpse by now. He felt showing respect for the dead seemed a ridiculous lie in the face of what he was doing to the living. He wished he had covered it up.

Guilt

Wednesday, July 3rd, 1984: Fairhaven, Massachusetts

Tom had made his last pick-up and was headed for Finger's house when the Fairhaven police pulled him over. Before the first officer got out of his car a second, and unmarked, car arrived and pulled in front of Tom's truck. Tom rolled down his window as the uniformed officer approached from behind.

"License and registration, please."

Tom had his driver's license ready and handed it to the policeman. When he leaned over to get the registration from the glove box, he saw another officer standing on the passenger side. The policeman shifted back and directed the beam of his flashlight on Tom through the glass. His elbow was back in the draw position. Tom opened the glove box and got the vehicle registration from under his tape measure. The officer on the driver's side took the registration with his left hand. His right hand was on his gun.

"Sir, your vehicle matches the description of a suspect. We need to search your vehicle."

"Am I under arrest?"

"Not unless you refuse to let us search your vehicle. Please step out of the vehicle and wait on the curb with Officer Wilhoit."

Officer Wilhoit stepped around in front of Tom's truck and motioned for Tom to stand by the front bumper. He did so and allowed himself to be patted down. The other officer searched the pickup briefly and came out with the brown paper bag from Bobby. The rest of the cash was hidden behind the door panel.

"Is this your bag, sir?"

"Yes."

"What's in the bag, sir?"

"Some cash and a deposit ticket."

The officer placed the paper bag in a larger plastic bag. "We need you to answer some questions."

Tom nodded. "I guess I'm not being arrested unless I refuse to go downtown with you."

"That's correct, sir."

Officer Wilhoit walked up to the rear passenger door of the unmarked car. He opened it and motioned for Tom to get in the back seat. Tom looked at his pickup.

"Don't worry about that."

Tom got into the unmarked car. The other officer handed the evidence bag to the driver of the unmarked car. The driver and the man who sat beside Tom in the backseat wore suits and did not speak.

When they arrived in front of the police station, the man in the backseat opened his door and got out. Leaning back in, he said, "Come with me."

Tom followed the man into the police station. The officer with him indicated Tom should sit on a bench, then went behind the concierge desk and began writing in his notebook. The other officer went into an office across the room.

A half hour later, the officer returned. "Detective Roche wants to speak to you." He held open the door to the back office.

Tom got up and went through the door. The officer went out. There were three desks in the room. A gaunt man in a brown leather jacket occupied one. The nameplate on the desk read “Detective Roche.” The lean man at the desk looked up. A clear plastic bag with the brown paper bag in it was on the man’s left. Theodore Roche got up and walked around the desk.

“You the night deposit man for the Ferry Café, are you?”

Tom looked at the yellow notepad on the desk and said, “Yes. I fix…repair stuff too.”

Detective Roche went back behind his desk. He retrieved a photograph from under the yellow pad. Still standing, he held it up to Tom. “You know this guy?”

“Yes, but not really.”

“He’s the…night deposit man for another business in town.”

“Probably,” Tom said.

“How about this guy?” Detective Roche stepped forward, grasping another photo in both hands, but watching Tom. It was the photograph of a dead man with a largish hole in his forehead. Tom frowned as he examined the photograph.

“No…no, I don’t know him.”

“Never met him?”

“No. For real, I never met or seen him.”

“You don’t seem surprised to see a man with his brains running out. Are you used to that?”

“Yeah. I guess I am.”

Detective Roche placed the photograph between them on the desk then took a few steps around the desk and looked at Tom's shoes, his legs, his stomach, his hands, then his eyes.

"You ever kill anyone, Tom?"

Tom met his gaze then looked down. "Yes. Yes, I have." He looked at the top of the desk. "In Nam."

"Did you like it?"

Tom jerked his head up. "No! Of course I didn't."

Roche nodded and said, "More than once?"

"Yes, more than once."

"You understand if you've killed more than once, I'm thinking you could kill again."

"Yeah…so, you ever kill anyone, detective?"

Roche smiled. "Yeah." Then he looked at his notepad. Then back at Tom. "Yeah…and more than once. Still, you're a suspect. What can you tell me?"

Roche leaned back. His eyes narrowed and he waited.

Tell him what? What does he mean?

"I don't know *who* did it. I'm pretty sure who *didn't*."

Detective Roche folded his arms and nodded.

Tom continued. "Finger didn't. Maybe The Roach. Not Bobby or Finger."

"Why not Finger?"

Tom looked at Detective Roche. Roche eyed him back and said, "I mean, why *maybe* The Roach, but *not* Finger?"

Tom fidgeted. "OK. The beat-up guy, Hack, he works for Finger. Whoever beat him up took the money, which was Finger's." Tom looked at the notepad. Roche followed his gaze. He leaned forward, picked up the yellow pad and dropped it on the floor. Tom continued as he pointed to the photo of the dead man. "So maybe Finger found out this guy was the one who beat up Hack and stole his money."

"But?" Roche said.

"But…Bobby told me that Finger wasn't going to do anything. That he would let someone else take care of it. I believe Bobby. He's not violent like this." Tom tapped the photo of the corpse. "Bobby doesn't even want drugs in the neighborhood. There's another but. He's worried about something he's not saying." Tom looked at the dark doorway, which led to another room.

Roche moved his chair back. Leaning forward, he placed his arms on his knees. "The Roach is my little brother. I protect him, sometimes from himself."

Tom kept staring into the shadows and said, "You love your little brother?"

"Yes, I do."

Tom turned back toward the desk and laid his arms on it to support his weight. "Last Wednesday, when I got to the Ferry Café to see Bobby and pick up the uh…deposit. That's the first time he included a deposit ticket. He said just in case I need to explain the cash. Then he told me about Hack and how Finger wasn't going to do anything, let someone else take care of it. Then he told me that Finger said I should leave my .45—Not to get caught with it. So I gave it to The Roach. He locked it in his desk."

Detective Roche did not change expressions. He was looking at the floor.

"That's about it for me. I'm new on the block. So what about your brother?"

Detective Roche sat up, pursed his lips. "What about him?"

"Nothing. I don't know him. Well, he's hard. A brick wall. Does anybody know him?"

Detective Roche tapped his chest with his index finger. "I do."

Tom sat up straight and said, "So I don't know much more."

Detective Roche placed his hands palm down on the desk and looked at Tom. Tom started looking around the room at the other desktops, into the corners, the light fixtures, the windows and floor.

Detective Roche said, "I know your girlfriend bought the Blue Oyster. I heard when she bought the liquor license. I'm starting to wonder what else came with it."

"Like what has that got to do with this poor sap?" Tom flipped the corpse photo across the desk.

Roche said, "I'm thinking that people who did that are the ones who are wanting to control drugs in this town. Cocaine, mostly. The dead guy might be dealing without an organization. No plan. No protection—a loose cannon."

"You're guessing, Roche."

"I'm good at guessing, Tom." Roche picked up the yellow pad off the floor and tossed it on the desk, gathered the two photos, and slid them between the yellow sheets. He stood. "You won't be seeing your .45."

"No problem."

Detective Roche narrowed his eyes and said, "Would you use it, Tom?"

"I don't think I would."

"You sure about that, Tom?"

"No, not really. I like to think I wouldn't use it unless I really, unavoidably had to." Tom stood up.

"Yeah. Trouble is, Mr. Warden, you never know for sure until the opportunity arises." They looked at each other. "What I mean is, it takes practice not to shoot people. It takes more training to learn how *not* to pull the trigger than how *to* pull the trigger. You need to experience that more, Tom. Not pulling the trigger, I mean." Detective Roche sat down. "You got money for a taxi?" Roche tossed the brown bag to Tom. He caught it with both hands. Roche said, "Well, go on. Go. I'm not your shrink. Get out of here." Tom turned and left the back office.

As he passed the front desk, the officer on duty said, without looking up, "Goodnight, Shrub."

Tom walked three blocks before he found a phone booth and called a taxi, which took him to his truck. Then he drove back to Sarah's. It was midnight when he got there.

Tom entered the house as quietly as he could and checked the bedroom. Sarah was asleep. He went to the kitchen, got a beer and went out on the doorstep. *Almost a full moon.* Somebody's dog was snuffing its way up the side street. Tom lit a Marlboro, took a deep drag and said, "Well shit, now what?" He summed it up in his mind; *I'm a maybe murder suspect. The woman I'm in love with might be setting up to deal cocaine for the*

Patriarca family and I'm wondering how to learn how not to kill people. Then out loud, "I should have stayed in Indiana." *Maybe go visit mom and dad in Arizona. Bed, go to bed*. Tom finished his smoke and beer then went inside. He took off his boots before he went back to the bedroom. Sarah stirred when he slid under the covers, then she rolled toward him, pulled his arm to her and fell back into a deep sleep. At that moment moving away from Sarah didn't seem like a good idea.

Tom slept. Exhausted. Finger's money lay on the floor beside the bed. He was conscious of the .45 automatic missing from under his pillow. Dreams came. Dreams went. He felt like his life had been spent. The long days and longer nights strung out into the past and future. He hoped his dreams would be kind tonight. His mind drifted, *Weeds are flowers that grow too well and have not learned their place to dwell. I'm a weed…*

Angels

Thursday, July 4th, 1984: Fairhaven, Massachusetts

"You were late last night." Sarah stood in the bedroom door in her bathrobe drying her hair with a towel. Tom rolled over.

"Morning, Sarah." Sarah leaned against the doorframe and waited. Tom pushed himself up in bed and said, "I told you how Bobby was worried I might get stopped. Well, I did, and I got to talk to a Detective Roche about the shooting. The body belonged to the guy who beat up Hack, I think. At least Hack's bag of money was in the car with him." Tom reached down and picked up the brown bag from the floor. "This is the pick-up from Bobby." He set the bag on the nightstand, got up, put on his jeans, and sat back on the bed. "I felt I could trust Detective Roche."

"Did you tell the detective all that?"

"Well, yes. I just felt I could trust him."

"You know The Roach, Bobby's cook, is Theo Roche's younger brother."

"Yeah, he told me. What's the story behind the detective, anyway?"

Sarah sat on the end of the bed. "Well, he's from around here. He lives on the top floor of a three-decker. His parents are dead. Never met them."

"Do you know him at all?"

Sarah smiled, looking up at the wall. "He arrested me for drunk driving my senior year in high school.

Most of the kids got away with it back then. They'd get stopped and the police officer would follow them home and that was it. But not Roche. He had the Mustang my dad gave me impounded and locked me up for the weekend. I had to walk five blocks to school for a week. Actually, I ran. I felt special because I'd spent time in jail and maybe because Detective Roche cared enough to lock me up."

"So, did that teach you a lesson?"

"Well, for a while. I started drinking again in college. I mean, I always drank, but I started getting drunk again. That's how I broke my collarbone. I got drunk and ran into a tree. A big fucking tree. I almost died." She looked at the floor. "Anyway, I was telling you about Detective Roche. He was in the Korean War. Maybe that's what clicked with you. Both war vets."

She looked at Tom, reached over, and shook his knee. "I never really thought of that. There *is* something different about you guys." Sarah sat a moment, picking at a hangnail. "I'm thinking of all the guys I know that have been to war, and yes, you're different." She took his hand. "That must be a hard thing to live with, but don't ask me to understand, because I can't."

Tom squeezed her hand, "All right. Sarah, I won't, but I wish you could. I really wish you could."

Sarah pulled free, put her hands on her knees and pushed herself up. "Well, let's get going. We got chickens to hatch and eggs to fry." She clapped her hands, "Chop, chop." She strode to her closet.

Tom headed for the bathroom and showered. Standing at the sink, he lit a cigarette, flipped on the exhaust fan, and shaved while he smoked. He was worried about his .45. The hole in the victim's head looked like an exit wound from a .45. Could his have been used in the murder? Had The Roach used it himself and could use it to frame him? Could he trust Detective Roche to believe Tom had actually given up his gun before the murder? Tom figured he could trust Detective Roche to take care of his own brother. Maybe he'd ask The Roach for the gun back. He hoped it was still there.

It was eleven o'clock by the time Tom and Sarah got to the Blue Oyster. He set up the new hot water rinse rack and installed the on-demand water heater required by the health department. Tom was putting trim around a window in the dining area when two men came in. One in jeans and golf shirt, the other in slacks and crew-neck sweater. The man in the sweater looked at Tom and said, "Sarah here?"

Tom motioned with his hammer. "In the office." The man continued past Tom and through the door that led to the kitchen. The golf shirt pulled a chair from one of the tables and sat. Tom completed the window trim and started on its partner. About twenty minutes passed. The sweater walked from the back and out the front door. The golf shirt followed, leaving the chair where he had set it.

Tom set a couple nails and put his tools down. He walked toward the office. The door was open. He went back to the front door and flipped the deadbolt to the locked position. On his way back to the office, he got himself a cup of coffee and lit a cigarette.

Sarah was typing something. Tom set his coffee on a table under the only window in the office. He opened the bathroom-sized window and blew smoke at it. He watched a bird sitting in the bushes that grew in the alley. Sarah typed. Tom smoked.

Finally Tom said, "Those two friends from college, Sarah?"

"Maybe it's better if you don't know."

"Better for who? Me, you, your two friends?"

Sarah let out a good laugh. "OK, better for me. Easier for me." She looked over at Tom. "You don't need to be involved in my whole life."

"Fine," Tom went back to the dining area and spoke to the empty room. "I guess we won't be getting married," Tom said to himself.

They really hadn't talked about getting married. They talked about married life, how other people handled marriage, but not their own possibility of marriage. They talked a lot about money, how other people handled money, but not about the possibility of them making a life together. The voice in Tom's mind mumbled, *Not possible, not possible, not going to happen.*

Tom knew he should go back to work on the window trim, but stood over his tools, unable to pick them up. He could not see the point. He wanted to smash something.

"Why can't I have that?" he said under his breath. "Why?" He unlocked the front door. Wanted to leave—to run. The voice again. Run where? To what? From what?

He picked up his tape measure and remembered the time he almost picked up a compass lying in a rice paddy before he saw the tripwire attached. It was a shit job for a booby-trap. He remembered how he disarmed it, and wondered why he didn't blow it in place. Yet it had done its job. It slowed them down enough to make them hurry to get to the LZ. It's not a good idea to be in a hurry in a booby-trapped area. Tom was staring out the front window thinking how he would have put the trip wire *away* from the compass so a man would trip it while reaching for the compass.

"What are you thinking about, Tom?" Sarah stood in the kitchen doorway. He stood in the middle of the room, staring at the tape measure in his hand. He stood still until the tape measure changed from a compass back into what it really was, then wondered why he had a tape measure in his hand. "You OK, Tom?"

Tom spoke to the tape measure. "No. I'm not OK."

"What's wrong?"

"I don't know."

Sarah walked toward him and said, "Look, it's not that I don't trust you, but there are just some things I can't tell you about the business."

"What?"

"I can't tell you everything."

Tom clipped the tape measure to his belt. "Why not? It wouldn't change how I feel about you."

Sarah stopped about four feet from Tom. "Well…how do you feel, Tom?"

"I feel like I can't tell you everything."

"Why not?"

"It would change the way you feel about *me*. Like now. Like why I can't work. Can't. I can't measure a length and remember it long enough to mark a board." Tom looked past Sarah. "It was a shit job for a trip wire."

"What?"

"Nothing."

Sarah raised her hands slightly, palms facing Tom, and said, "Nothing was a shit job? That's great, Tom."

He looked at the floor, unclipped the tape measure from his belt and tossed it toward his toolbox. It clattered to a stop against the wall. Sarah stepped a little closer.

"Tom…I've been seeing a counselor…about some things. I think…she could help you…if you went to see her." Tom's stare went from outside the window to Sarah's eyes. His mouth pulled tight. Sarah took another step closer.

"I'm not saying you're crazy, but I can't live with this. You're my lover. You work for me. You're 'Tom', then you're somebody else. You disappear for days." Sarah lowered her hands and placed her palms against her thighs. "Just talk to the counselor. OK?"

Sarah took a step closer. Tom clenched his fists and stepped back. Sarah couldn't see his eyes. She took a step back, turned and went to the office. She found a business card in her purse and went back to the dining area. Without stopping, she walked up to Tom and held out the card. Softly she said, "Just talk to her…Please?"

Tom took the card and stared at it. "Yes, Sarah. I will." He stood there, staring at the card. Sarah went back to her office. She looked back to check on him, then closed her office door.

Tom stared at the card without seeing it. He wanted to scream. He stared at the card. He wanted to break something. He stared at the card. He knew if he moved his eyes the first thing he saw would be destroyed. If he moved, he would be destroyed. If he took a step, he would die. He knew he had to move. He always had to move, even if it meant dying. He had to move. Why wouldn't his feet move? *Move! Move now! Move now!*

He breathed. His hands loosened. His arms dropped. The haze closed him in. His knees unlocked.

"Let it go," he said. "Let it go."

It was safe to look at the floor. Then move his arms. Tom put the card in his hip pocket and stepped toward his toolbox, then turned toward the front door and shuffled toward it. He made a careful exit. Getting in his pickup, he drove around back and parked it in the alley behind the bar.

***

Sarah sat at her desk and tried to focus on business. She could not. Her thoughts followed her heart back to four years ago when she first met Tom. She remembered it was at Mike's Italian Restaurant. She noticed him and sent him a drink at the bar. She remembered being a little surprised when he responded by coming over to the booth where she and her friend were sitting. He sat down facing her and said, "Mind if I sit down?"

She had laughed, and then they talked and talked. When her friend left, they stayed talking and exchanged phone numbers. She called him first, but Tom couldn't meet. He called her next and they met for lunch at the tennis club where she was a member. The following Sunday, they met for breakfast and spent the day together. That night they went back to the beach house he rented in Mattapoisett. It was October. He built a fire in the fireplace and they made love on the bearskin rug in front of the fireplace. It stayed beautiful for them for several weeks. She felt the deep affection between them growing, but was afraid to call it love.

She remembered when he first became aware of the intimacy between them. He seemed bewildered, then cautious. She couldn't say exactly when the lovemaking became only sexual satisfaction, but before a year passed, the loving man she knew that first night had shut himself off and hidden from her. Somehow that seemed normal. It seemed as if that was the way it would be for her.

Now she was beginning to understand that his emotional retreat had more to do with him than her. She was frustrated and sad and determined that she would win. *If I only knew what winning looks like.* She wished her two older brothers were there with her now. She knew that wasn't possible, not like it used to be. They were both married and had families. One lived in Hawaii, the other in Japan. They had treated her like a brother growing up, so it was understandable she understood boys better than girls. She had the confidence of a man and the vulnerability of a woman. She was beginning to understand that a man's confidence was not a substitute for a woman's confidence.

***

Tom was still in his truck parked in the alley behind the Blue Oyster when he woke up. The daylight made him squint and shield his eyes. He found a warm beer under the seat, popped the top and drank some, lit a cigarette, and lay back against the driver's side door. *I should go back to work.* "Fuck it. It don't mean nuthin'."

He remembered Sarah asking him how he felt. *I feel nothing.* Tom thought about getting his gun from the glove box. He would feel safer if it was in his hand or lying in his lap. Then he remembered he'd given the .45 to The Roach. He wanted it back. "Fuck," he said aloud. "Fuck me. Fuck it. It don't mean nuthin'." *Just drive, just drive away. That always works.* He remembered riding his bike the mile and a half to the fishing hole and walking down to the creek. Opening another beer, he closed his eyes, and drifted back to a time before it all went wrong.

Two hours later, he woke up. Checked his wristwatch. Almost 4 o'clock. He opened the pickup door and put one leg out. After about a minute, he stepped out and took a drink from the water jug in the truck bed. Sarah's car was gone. Tom used his key to get back into the Blue Oyster, where he used the bathroom. Then used the big kitchen sink to flood his head with water. The same thoughts continued their invasion. *Fuck me. Fuck it. It don't mean nuthin'.* The truth was, Sarah did mean something to him. Right then he couldn't say that he loved her. He needed her. He felt OK with her. He had no real hope he could change, but Sarah wanted him to call Mara Selby, the therapist.

He ignored the rumbling and tumbling in his mind as much as he could and went to the office and called the therapist. She had an opening next Friday. He made the appointment and hung up the phone. A blank minute passed then he said, "Time to get some work done." He brewed some coffee and continued working on the repairs and upgrades that needed to be done for the Blue Oyster opening two weeks from Friday.

Head Games

Friday, July 19th, 1984: Boston, Massachusetts

On the way to his appointment with the therapist Tom started to feel like it was a long drive. Not long enough to get completely relaxed, but long enough to calm down, then get worked up about what he would say. So Tom was already getting angry when he walked into the therapist's office. "Good morning."

Mara looked up from her desk. "Hi. Are you Tom?"

"I was this morning."

"Well then, if you'll just fill out this form, we can get started. I'll be back in a few minutes."

Tom sat at the desk in the chair provided. He hated filling out forms, hated the questions–Any head injuries? Any history of mental illness in your family? Tom was writing one answer on the form and thinking of another.

I've heard stories about Grandpa. No, no diagnosis. An alcoholic aunt. An uncle who lives alone and doesn't speak. But no, no history of mental illness. What's bothering you? I don't like feeling like an ax murderer. They're just feelings, you're not going to act on them. No, but how long can I have those feelings and hold them back before I get too tired to resist and start accommodating those feelings just to get some relief? Make it stop! Make it stop! Can you make it stop? No, I can't. I want it to stop. I want to run screaming from the building. I want to be eaten by a tiger. I want to blaspheme. I want to hurt something. Fuck me! Fuck me! Fuck me!

Mara opened the door of her consultation room. “Come on in Tom. Have a seat.” Tom eased up out of the chair and closed his eyes for a moment. Walking up to her desk, he handed her the form he had filled out. She glanced at it and put it down. “So Tom, what’s going on?”

“Well, how do you mean?”

“How do you feel?”

“As little as possible.” Tom said, not quite smiling.

“Well, that’s hard sometimes.”

Tom looked at Mara, then at the floor. “Sarah recommended you.”

“Oh. I sometimes do couples counseling, but this isn’t about that specifically, is it?”

“No. Just…well. What’s troubling me is getting in the way of Sarah and I getting closer, I guess.”

“Umm?”

“It’s just that I understand Sarah. She talks about what’s troubling her and I help her. Mostly I just listen. I can’t talk to her about what troubles me. I’m not sure I can talk to you.”

“It’s a matter of trust, Tom.”

“You want me to trust you? I don’t know. You’re about to mess with my head. If you’re any good at it, you’ll have the skill to change that mess and I don’t know if you’re any better than I am at what my mind should be like. Anyway, I’m desperate and I’m absolutely no good at helping myself so, if Sarah trusts you, so do I.”

"OK. I'll be your last resort, so to speak, but understand, I'm a counselor, not a therapist. I can point out some things maybe you don't see about yourself."

"All right. What do we do? Talk? It's easier to talk to strangers. Family is hard, you know. They think of you the way they thought you were, and I'm different now."

"It wasn't so long ago that your family knew you, was it?"

"Well, let's see. I am thirty-eight, so about fifteen years I guess."

"How long have you been changed?"

"What? Changed? How long?"

"Yes, you indicated that what's bothering you was there before you met Sarah."

"Yeah, yeah. I thought Sarah would help me forget. Get over it."

"Get over what, Tom?"

"The war."

"You mean the Vietnam War?"

"Yeah. Nam. That one. And well…just can't say."

"That seems to fit I guess. Were you drafted?"

"Yep, but I could have stayed in college. Then I volunteered for special training."

"Umm?"

"So I can't say it was Nam, really. I mean why would being in combat make me afraid? Why would being in a war make me wish I were dead? We were trying so hard to survive. For Christ's sake, when I did survive, shouldn't I appreciate every minute of life?"

Mara waited. Tom looked around the room. "It wasn't that hard to kill people, you know. And then it got easier. It got easier to die, too. It was easy to accept death. Maybe that's it. I accepted my death and lived like I was already dead. That's the way we lived with fear, the constant threat of dying. I remember thinking, 'Hell, I'm not going to make it home. I'm going to die here in Nam. What difference does it make if I die today or next month?'

"But wasn't there anything you wanted to come home to?"

"Well, at first, yes, but thinking about the things I had to live for made dying that much harder. Especially when the shit hit the fan and you knew you were going to die in the next few minutes. The worst was patrolling in booby-trapped areas. Every step felt like it could be my last. Those were the times when I stopped thinking about the things I wanted to live for. Wanting to have the sweet things in life just made it too hard to die. So maybe I didn't see the whole picture, but at the time I figured I had to stop thinking about living or stop thinking about dying. I was in Nam. There was no fucking way I could stop thinking about dying…no way."

Mara took a breath. "You can go back to thinking about living now."

"That's the thing, God damn it. I didn't figure out how I stuffed my feelings inside till now. That's fifteen years after I got back. When I got back people would say, 'Well, you best forget about that, Tom.' Fuck you, forget it. Maybe that's what the flashbacks are for. So I can remember and figure out what to do, and no, I can't just start thinking about what there is to live for. And no, I can't help thinking I will be dead by next month. I don't think…"

Tom got up out of his chair and continued talking to the corner of the room. "It's not like I think I'm going to die or get killed. I just never picture myself being alive next month. Sometimes not even next week, or even tomorrow." Tom swung around to Mara. "That's what I'm talking about. Why I don't trust you." Tom advanced on Mara's desk, shouting. "You dredge this up and think you'll explain it to me and I'll be all better when I understand!" Tom gripped the front edge of the desk and tilted it back. "Well, I don't want to fucking understand my feelings! I don't want to get rid of them!"

Mara sat in her chair holding the desk pad to keep it from sliding off. She drew in a breath and said, "OK, Tom, put the desk down."

He looked at his hands gripping the edge of the desk.

"Oh," he said. He lowered the desk and went to pick up the things that had slid off the desk.

"No, that's all right, just walk it off."

"You mean like outside?" Tom moved toward the door.

"No, no, you're fine."

"I mean…just…just. I'm sorry," he said and slumped into the chair in front of the desk. Mara took a minute to straighten her desk and glanced at the clock.

"Tom, you know Sarah never described you as being, well, violent or aggressive. I mean with her. How about with friends?"

"Don't have any."

"Well, people you work with."

Tom took a moment. "I can feel the anger coming. So before that happens I just leave, go off by myself and let the black rage come."

"Is that why you list twenty different jobs in the last fifteen years?"

"Ya mostly, but sometimes it's 'cause I get good at my job, then the boss expects me to be good at my job all the time, then I get a spell where I can't concentrate. I can't stop thinking about the war, then drink at night to make it stop. Then I can't do the job. The boss is unhappy and I leave before he has to fire me. I had this one boss in a cabinet shop. His older brother was a vet. He helped me. He'd give me a long weekend or maybe Wednesday off. He understood. He gave me ten days once. It was his shop and he could do what he wanted, not like a regular job. I can't keep a regular job. It's like most of the time I have two hands, but several times a year I show up with an arm missing and the boss finally says 'Fuck off.' Women understand, like when they're pregnant and need a few months off they should have their job back when they're ready. And besides…"

"Excuse me, but our time is up, Tom."

"Time?"

"Yes. You've given me a lot, don't you think?"

"Ya, I guess so."

"Well, there are some things I can help you with and some things I can't. I just want you to know you are not crazy. Not at all. You're getting a handle on your life. Probably doesn't feel like it, but you are. It probably doesn't seem fair, but what is it you Vietnam vets say? Fuck it. It don't mean nuthin'?"

He laughed and said, "Yeah, that's it. Fuck it, it don't mean nuthin'." Tom laughed a little more, then his eyes filled with tears. Mara came around the desk with some tissue. Tom took two. "Maybe I can be alive again. Just maybe I can."

Mara put an appointment card in his hand and let him out the side door. That way the person going out didn't have to meet the person coming in.

Tom almost skipped back to his pickup. He hopped into the driver's seat. "Ha ha-a-a, I'm going to get better." He took several deep breaths to slow the process. He knew he could come down as fast as he went up. He watched himself in order to savor the happy feelings. He didn't understand what brought them yet, but Mara could help with that or maybe she knew someone who could. Tom couldn't remember if Mara was scared or not. *Maybe I'm not so bad if she wasn't afraid of me when I lost it there for a minute.* Tom turned on the radio and spoke to the music, "Hey maybe I'm not such a badass after all." Tom smoothed the manic high into a feeling of wellbeing. He had learned that it was more practical to feel good for a week than to feel like a king for a day.

When he got back to New Bedford, it was time to make the rounds picking up money from the bookies.

Trip Wire

April, 1969, Republic of South Vietnam

Alpha Company was clearing an area near a bridge. They knew there were booby-traps there, but they had to go in and search for weapon caches. When that was done, they would sweep both sides of the canal, looking for VC. Two platoons were sent west from the bridge where they would set up blocking positions on each side of the canal. A platoon from Alpha Company and an ARVN platoon we're going to sweep each side of the canal, moving toward the two blocking platoons-the old *hammer and anvil* tactic. Nice name. Sometimes it was a hamburger and chopping block tactic.

Sgt. Warden's platoon had one side of the river. The ARVN's had the other. They went in with three squads. All three point men wore extra flack-skirts to protect their legs. Within the first fifty feet, the first squad point man tripped a booby trap. He got hit in the hand with a piece of bamboo and was able to walk back up to the road. Another ten feet and third squad tripped one. Somehow the point man had missed it, and the second man hit the wire. It killed him and wounded the guy next to him. They didn't move for about ten minutes while third squad got the dead and wounded back up to the road. Not so easy. They had penetrated into the booby-trapped area and the point men had missed some wires. So now the guys carrying the dead man in a poncho were thinking about the trip wires the point man had passed. They were good at following in the steps ahead of them, but this was different.

When the dust-off choppers left and first and third squad got back up, Sgt. Warden knew it was time to move. All this time he was thinking about his high school sweetheart, wanting to see her again before he died. Tom was thinking about how hard it would be to go fishing if he lost a leg before noon today.

Warden walked second and was watching the point man. Usually he'd walk third, even fourth, back with the machine gunner, but today he was taking his share of the risk. It was time to move and Donald, the point man from Minnesota, was turned around facing him. Tom hoped the fear didn't show on his own face like it did on the point man's. Donald didn't look down in shame or anything like that. He just looked at Warden straight and said, "I don't want to die, Sarge."

Warden needed to take a step. It was then he put all thoughts of home in a box and buried the things he wanted to live for. He stepped toward Donald who just kept looking at Tom with pleading eyes. He took another step. He was going to take point. *Fuck it. I haven't got anything to live for anyway.*

Before he made it all the way up to Donald, the company commander gave the order to pull back. The CO had decided to get some mobile antiaircraft guns to fire point-blank into the area along the river to explode any remaining booby-traps and go back in afterwards.

The next day, on their second attempt, they made it through and moved upriver. Nobody else found a trip wire. Donald didn't die. Sgt. Warden didn't die, but he stopped thinking about the things he wanted to live for. Wanting to live just made it too hard to die.

The Ferry Café

Wednesday, August 7th, 1984: Acushnet, Massachusetts

There was plenty of time to get something to eat before he made his pick-up at Call Me Ishmael's, a bakery in the historic district. He swung the pickup in behind the Ferry Café then walked around and through the front door. Bobby was busy behind the counter. Louise was waiting table. Tom took the corner booth and caught her attention. Louise made her way over to Tom, refilling coffee cups on the way.

She set the coffee carafe down. "Hey Tom, how ya doin'?"

"I'm good. You good?"

"Sure, sweetie."

"I'm hungry for a burger and fries. Lettuce, tomato and onion. Extra mayo."

"Anything ta drink?"

"Root beer."

"All right sweetheart, burger, fries, root beer."

The Ferry Café was half full of a supper crowd and everybody was talking loud enough for everyone else in the place to hear them. Tom figured that New Englanders always talked loud enough for everyone in the room to hear them, even if it was a restaurant. Well, almost all the time. Tom salted and peppered his fries and drenched them with catsup. He finished and ordered pie and coffee. Bobby made a good *cuppa joe*. Tom was on a coffee refill and Marlboro when Bobby came over.

"How you doin', Shrub?"

"Good, Bobby, you all right?"

"Sure," Bobby said while sliding into the booth. He spread his hands on the tabletop. "How you and Sarah doin'?"

Tom shrugged. "We have our ups and downs. She ain't going to marry me, though."

"Is that 'cause you ain't going to ask, or 'cause she's going to say no?"

"Both are right."

"Aw, come on, Tom. You don't know what she'd say. Anyway, with a girl like Sarah, you got to ask more than once. Even after you're married, you got ta keep asking."

"Well, I'm not the most—what—stable guy in the world. I like my time alone."

"Yeah, well, you can be alone with someone."

Tom sipped his coffee and looked around the restaurant. "She's going to take a chance with the Blue Oyster, I think."

"Yeah, that's not a good thing. But no need to worry. The girl's smart."

"Umm, she's not talking to me about it." He gave Louise a nod as she set a piece of apple pie in front of him. "You know she got a visit from some strangers. Two guys. One wears a golf shirt and jeans, the other slacks and crewneck sweater. The golf shirt is about mid-50s, thick neck, shaved head. The guy wearing slacks and crewneck is like thirty-nine, early forties. Athletic, neat as a pin."

"Sounds like a lot of guys. I'll ask around. Tell me more about these guys, Shrub."

"They came in the Oyster and talked to Sarah alone. Well, the crewneck did. The other guy watched me. She wouldn't say what they wanted. Said I didn't need to know." Tom rested his fingertips on the table's edge.

Bobby nodded. "It hurts when they have secrets, don't it, Tom?" Tom nodded. "You tell her that?" Tom shook his head no. "You just let it be, didn't you? You didn't push or question, did ya?"

"Well, I started to. It was going to end in an argument. What good would that do? I just dropped it."

"So? I argue with Mary all the time. We ain't mad or nothing like that, but we argue. If you don't argue with them they think you don't love 'em. Sides, making up is fun. You know what I mean?"

Tom looked up. "No, I don't. I sort of do, but no, not really. Sometimes arguments can get out of hand. Go too far and then there's no making up."

Bobby was watching the counter. "Just a sec." Bobby got up and went to the cash register and rang up a few sales.

Tom watched him. He liked Bobby. Everybody liked Bobby. They knew who he was. Bobby knew who he was and what he wanted. Bobby enjoyed doing whatever he was doing. *How does that happen? Some people are lucky. No, that isn't true. Bobby set it up this way. Somehow he decided to be happy. He's OK with being Bobby. More than that, he's OK with you being you*. Bobby was back at the booth. He slapped Tom's shoulder then swung in to the opposite seat.

"Don't be so glum, Shrub. It ain't all bad. Life is full of surprises. Good and bad surprises. You just have to ask. You just have to let them come, all of them." Bobby sat back and looked out across the diner, then looked back at Tom. "Yeah, OK. Look, Tom, I ain't one to give advice. I'm not saying you're doing it wrong, but you could just try something different."

"Well, I don't know. It ain't safe. You know, let well enough alone."

"Geez, OK, look. I'm just going to tell you. Why don't you just ask Sarah to marry you?"

"What? You ask her."

"You want to leave her?"

"No."

"You want to stay with her?"

"Yes."

"You want to stay with her just the way things are?"

"No."

"Well, being married would be different." Bobby sat back and scanned the room. Tom ate his pie and drank coffee.

Two men in slacks and polo shirts came in and sat at the bar. Bobby watched them. Tom leaned out and motioned to Louise for more coffee and checked for what got Bobby's attention. When Tom turned back Bobby asked, "Same two guys talked to Sarah?"

"Yep. same two guys."

"They work for Patriarca. Loyal men, those two. Strictly business. Like angels, messenger angels.

Nothing personal." Bobby grabbed the outside edge of the booth. "Hey, I got to make myself valuable. I'll get your baklava and coffee to go." Bobby slid out of the booth, turned, and rested one hand on the tabletop and one hand on Tom's shoulder. "Think about what I said about Sarah. It's more important than all the rest of the crap going on in your head."

Bobby took care of business. In a few minutes Louise brought Tom a coffee to go and baklava. "Take care now," she said.

"Thanks, Lou." Tom dropped a twenty on the table and walked out without looking at anyone. It was time to make a money pickup across the harbor in New Bedford at Ishmael's. Tom had to wait for the bridge at Pope's Island to open. There was only one trawler passing so it didn't take long.

Ishmael's was a coffee shop and bakery. On other nights he would pick up the lists of numbers from one of Sarah's bookies. He never picked up the money and number lists at the same time. He got off Route 6. It took a few turns to get over to Acushnet Avenue, because all the streets were here a long time before Route 6 was even planned. Now he was in the historic district of New Bedford and it gave Tom a sense of being suspended in time, part of something larger. His reverie didn't last. A feeling from the here and now slipped in.

He still missed having the loaded .45 automatic pistol with him. He still felt threatened from all the corners of the world. That weapon represented his need to defend himself. He wondered if the time would ever come when a loaded gun was no longer a symbol, but just a tool. He still felt like a soldier, and yet wanted to lay aside the tools of violence. Only a warrior could do that. In the space between his thoughts, Tom Warden heard an inner voice he did not recognize as his own. The quiet voice told him, *A soldier deals in death. A warrior deals with life.*

Tom parked a half block from Union Street and walked to the corner. He had some time to kill so he turned left toward the waterfront. The construction job that brought him to New Bedford was on this block. When that job was over, he hadn't gone back to Indiana. He picked up other construction work and then found a steady job at the Whitehorse nuclear power plant. That steady job lasted about six months, then he just quit. It was then that he met Sarah at Mike's Italian restaurant near Mattapoisett.

It all seemed very random to Tom, like his life had no direction. He just ended up places. Like right now. He had walked all the way down Mac Arthur Drive and was standing in front of the old Bourne Counting House. The three-story granite building was built in the mid nineteenth century. Most of the whale oil from that era came through this building. Now it was a bed and breakfast. He looked up at the third floor where he'd spent his first week in New Bedford.

Tom turned and headed back toward Union Street as he tried to connect the dots of his life. It all made sense, up until the day he set foot in Vietnam. After that there was no pattern, no purpose, only a skimming of life. He walked back to Call Me Ishmael where he would pick up money.

As he approached the three steps leading up into Ishmael's, he put on a smile and went in. He felt better instantly. It seemed as if everyone there were friends or about to become friends. Becky, the owner, was ringing up a customer. He said, "Hi, Becky." She nodded.

When Tom scanned the customers, he saw Sarah's aunt, Laura, occupying a table for two near the front window. It took him half a second to register that she had been watching him before he took the four steps to her table.

Laura made some space at the table and shifted her chair. "Hello, Tom. How are you and Sarah?"

"OK, I guess." Sitting, Tom said, "You talk to her this week?"

"No, not for a while."

He took another look around the coffee shop, heaved a breath, and let his full weight settle into the chair. Tom spoke to Sarah as if they had been talking all afternoon. "She talks about you sometimes. I think you were her favorite aunt."

"I *am* her favorite aunt." Laura eyed Tom and said, "You said that like she had gone away forever."

"Yeah, sure, sorry I–" He looked at the front windows.

The banter in the coffee shop made their silence less awkward. Laura finished her tea. Smiling she touched his arm. "Tell Sarah she can call me."

Tom gave her a closed-lip smile. "Yes, yes, I will.

Becky came up to them and handed Tom a small brown paper bag. “Here’re your muffins, Tom.”

“Thanks. We’ll have these for dessert. Tom turned to Laura. “Sarah eats the muffin tops and leaves me the stumps.” Laura waited for the rest of the story. Tom got up from the table and left the coffee shop.

By the time he realized he had missed the turn onto Sconticut Neck Road, he was almost in Mattapoisett. He turned around and headed for Sarah’s house on West Island.

Sarah was slicing a cucumber and munching a carrot when Tom came in through the side kitchen door and said, “Late supper?”

“How you doing, Shrub?”

Tom grinned, handed her the bag of muffins and said, “You’re not supposed to know my undercover name.”

“Bobby let it slip.” Sarah took the muffins and a thick packet of money wrapped in waxed paper from the bag. She tossed the money toward the end of the counter and slid the cucumber slices off the cutting board onto the lettuce. She began slicing a tomato. “Make some garlic dressing …and be quick about it.”

“Yes, dear.”

Sarah tossed the chef’s knife onto the counter. “Don’t call me dear.”

“Yes, dear.” Tom chuckled. Sarah picked up the knife and carved a tomato. Tom pulled off a couple cloves of garlic, peeled the skin, and positioned himself at the counter next to Sarah, just close enough to get in her elbow room. He began to mash the garlic in the white porcelain mortar.

"Must you?"

"What?"

Sarah used the chef's knife to push the mortar about a foot farther away from her. Tom added salt and mint and worked the mixture.

Sarah said, "Did you talk to Bobby about those two visitors I had last week?"

"Maybe. We talk about a lot of things."

Sarah held the bottle of olive oil high over the glass bowl and drizzled oil onto the salad. Reaching over Tom, she picked up an onion and placed it on the cutting board. Sarah gave Tom a glance, went to the fridge, and picked up a lemon.

She placed it in the mortar in front of Tom and said, "Squeeze this." She turned back to her cutting board and continued. "Bobby is a smart man…a good man. We've been friends since high school."

"I think it's great to still live in the town you grew up in. Makes you feel like you have a place in the world. Like you belong."

"It's not all that great," Sarah said.

"But you never moved."

"No. Where would I go? What would be any different? Anyway, it's not like I haven't traveled around. I taught a girl's camp in Florida for three summers. I visit Julie in New York."

"Yeah, Julie. That was a fun trip when we went to her wedding last year. I felt kind of awkward. You know, like an outsider around all your friends from college at the reception."

"Yeah, you should have. They thought you were a hick, but a real genius hick." Sarah turned back to the cutting board. "Julie invited us to come stay with them and take in a play sometime."

"Yeah? OK." Tom picked up the mortar and stepped closer to pour the mixture of garlic, mint, and lemon over the salad. Sarah reached over his arm and cleaned the mortar with her finger then she sampled the savory juices left on her finger.

"Excellent job, Mr. Shrub." Sarah threw her head back and laughed. Took the mortar from Tom's hand and relished the remnants. "Let's eat." Tom set plates on the table. Sarah slid baked salmon from the oven.

"Want some wine?" Sarah asked, waving a bottle of Chianti. "Bobby gave it to us…me."

"Yea, I'd like some wine."

Sarah poured. They sat and ate. Sarah was an intense eater. She paid attention to and savored each mouthful. Tom followed her example. It was better than the almost ravenous way he usually ate. Tom never felt hungry, then all of a sudden he had to eat. He felt like a starving lion chewing on an antelope. When they had finished the late supper, Sarah started to get up with her empty plate.

Tom said, "I got that."

Sarah let him take her plate and settled back in her chair. He very seldom did something for Sarah without her asking. She didn't like it. Sarah folded her hands in her lap and waited for Tom to clear and rinse the plates. Tom closed the water faucets and spoke to the sink. "I wish we could stay together like this." He waited a second for Sarah to say something. When she didn't, he turned around and leaned back against the sink. Sarah was looking at her hands. Tom continued. "I mean…well, I guess we are staying together, but I can't shake the feeling it's going to end. Not in a disaster, but just drifting."

"I know," she said, then turned her head and spoke to him. "Can't we just do what we're doing? I'm OK with that."

"Well, it's OK, Sarah, but we could be *more* than OK." Sarah shifted her chair. "I mean…We could have a family. Always be together." Tom looked at the floor. "When I say it, it doesn't sound possible…but I want that. I want to have children with you." Tom looked up and held Sarah's eyes. "I don't know why, but I think it would make everything all right again.

Sarah looked away and said, "I don't want to have children…ever."

Tom began wiping down the kitchen. When he finished he began looking for something else to wipe clean. Thinking better of it, he tossed the sponge in the sink.

"Maybe you're right. It doesn't seem fair to expose children to someone like me. I guess I don't really want to, but still I think we should have children. I think I could make myself be all right."

"What? You don't want to have children. Why would you do something you don't want to if you have a choice? I mean. Mom thinks I should get married and have children, but I'm not going to just because she thinks I should."

"You should though."

"Why should I?"

"Well, you'd be a really fine mom, for one thing."

"Bullshit. I'd be a terrible mom. I would neglect my daughter."

Tom pushed himself away from the sink. "Your daughter? You want a little girl?"

Sarah's lips tightened and she pressed her knuckles to her mouth. Tom moved closer, then stood behind her so she could hide her feelings more easily. He rested his hands on Sarah's shoulders. "We don't have to talk about this now. I guess I'm not a very good candidate for a father. Can't hold a job, get angry, confused—disappear. But if you want, I'll marry you and help you raise kids."

Tom let his hands slip from her shoulders. He padded out the front door and sat on the steps. His hands shook a bit as he lit a Marlboro. He felt like crying, but couldn't. He only *felt* like crying and was pleased he could feel at least that. He smoked. This was one of those times he wished he could just fall asleep and never wake up. That somehow didn't seem like suicide, not even like dying. He was starting to feel again, and wasn't sure it was something he wanted to do.

The first feeling to come back was a malignant sadness, an aching for a life he had no hope of ever living. Then the anger came and threatened to become a black rage. It felt like the same rage he summoned on the battlefield in order to kill a fellow human being. The black dog had caught up to him again. He wanted a rifle in his hand, to feel its recoil, to see red tracer rounds streaking from it. He wanted to feel the thunder of artillery as the shrapnel ripped through an unseen enemy. He wanted to die anonymously on the battlefield. In all his confusion, he knew only one thing. All he was good for was being a soldier. Being one of the men who pulled the trigger so others wouldn't have to.

Now the tears did come, silently. He trapped a sob in his throat where it became an aching. He began the numbing process, but it wasn't enough. He gathered all his horror and despair and retreated with it until he became one of the hollow-eyed men. When he had lost nearly all feeling, he knew it was safe to move again. He got a beer from the cooler in his pickup and sat on the tailgate to drink it. He smoked, finished the beer, then went back into the house and locked the door. He looked at the couch in the living room, considered sleeping there, then continued to the bedroom. The hall light washed in. Sarah was in bed, facing the wall. Tom sat in the chair to take off his boots. He undressed and pulled on pajama bottoms and slipped into bed. It was not a conscious thought, but Tom Warden knew he would never have children with the woman he loved. It was a decision made in darkness.

Finger's Basement

Sunday August 18th, 1984: New Bedford, Massachusetts.

"Hey Finga, ya gonna put some felt on that table? It's gettin' kind of slick, don't ya think?" Lenny The Roach asked. The Roach sat at a card table in the corner of Finger's basement eating a salami sandwich. Finger was shooting pool with Detective Roche. It was really a half basement, with windows just above ground level. The pool table was an early Brunswick—dark wood, almost black.

Finger said, "I'll put on new felt when you pay for my skiff you sunk last summer."

"Was that yours? I thought it was your girlfriend's."

"Don't talk with your mouth full, Lenny," Roche said.

Lenny took a big bite, chewed once, and said, "Sure thing, Theo." Finger smiled.

Roche called, "Six ball, corner."

Finger said, "What was you thinkin', Roach, tryin' to haul a side of beef across Mill Pond in a rowboat?"

"Sounded like a great idea at the time. Anyway, I almost rowed all the way before the freaking stern fell off. Close enough to pull the side of beef ashore anyway. The whole transom was rotted. I should sue you for sending me out in an unsafe vessel."

Finger laughed and said, "Nice shot, Detective."

"Speaking of nice shots, I'm getting nowhere with who shot Timmy Furtado in the back of the head. I can't have that in my town." Roche turned directly toward Finger.

Finger took a step back. "I swear to God, Detective, I didn't ask anybody to do that. Whoever did it only got a couple grand. That ain't worth killing somebody over."

"You sure your friends on the Hill didn't do it out of courtesy?"

Finger answered, "Someone might have taken the two grand for themselves and roughed him up just to be friendly, but not kill the guy. Killing people has a price tag. Anyways, the guys on the Hill wouldn't leave a mess like that."

The Roach wiped his mouth with a hand towel. "Maybe it was a botched job."

"No," Roche said, "whoever did it meant to do it just like that."

Lenny said, "What about Shrub? He's capable of doing that."

Finger answered, "No, I don't think so. Why would he, anyway?"

"For the money, or just to send a message not to fuck with the bagman." Lenny washed down the last of the salami and provolone with beer.

Finger said, "I can't see Shrub doing it. He's a sweet guy."

"I'm not so sure," Roche said. "He looks guilty. You know? He's hiding something. And I don't care how sweet he is; he's a killer. He was an infantry sergeant in Nam and you don't just leave that behind. Killing gives you the mark of Cain. It stays with you forever."

Finger kissed the six ball, but missed the side pocket. "OK, Detective, just because he's capable doesn't mean he did. Besides, Bobby said he was in Kentucky." Finger pointed his cue at Roche. "You were in Korea and you don't kill for money or in some kind of rage."

"First of all, it was Indiana," Roche said. "I checked with the Indiana State Police to see what I could find out. Turns out that Tom Warden talked to an old neighbor who is now on the Indiana state police force on Sunday morning, June 23rd. And I know he got back here Wednesday night, June 26th. Timmy was killed Thursday night, June 27th. And he had a visit with Bobby at the Ferry Café late Thursday. You were thinking I didn't know that, weren't you? Anyway, that's not all that makes him a suspect. He's on my list because he feels guilty. That's all I'm saying." The detective pointed his pool cue at Finger. "You left something out about why men kill."

"Yeah? I thought that was all the reasons—kill for passion or money. Why else would a guy kill?"

"Because he likes it." Detective Roche slammed the cue ball into the seven and the seven slammed into the corner pocket.

Lenny got up. "Take it easy, Theo."

"Sure, Lenny, sure." Detective Roach lined up on the cue ball and made a smooth, light stroke. The cue ball kissed the eleven, then touched the rail just behind the eight-ball. Finger didn't have a shot.

"Thanks, Detective."

"You're welcome, Finger." Detective Roche stood with his legs apart, the butt of his cue stick on the floor between his feet, both hands gripping the shaft. He looked at Lenny and said, "You get immune to death. Ain't that right?"

Lenny sat back down in the chair next to the card table, rested his elbows on his knees and watched his older brother. Detective Roche kept looking at the empty area where Lenny was just standing. Finger waited. Theodore Roche spoke.

> When the red Chinese Army came down on us in Korea, we killed so many with thirty-caliber machine gun fire you could hardly see the ground out in front of our position. We stacked 'em up like cordwood. It made you feel like life was cheap, that death was no big deal. Like I said, a fellow can get to like killing. I still do, God help me. I'm not saying I do it for pleasure. Never did, but I like the power of it. The finality of it. You had to make a deal with the devil, though. You had to agree to be fair game. If you wanted to be a hunter, you also agreed to be the hunted. That's the deal. I thought it was a lifetime commitment, but I finally figured out I could cancel my contract with the devil anytime I wanted. That was a hard day for me. I always justified killing in the line of duty by saying a deal is a deal, even if it is with Satan. After that day, when I canceled my hunting license, I walked a fine line. I had to be exactly sure that when I drew my weapon it was for the right reason and not an excuse to do what I'd come to enjoy.

They finished the game in silence. Detective Roche held his cue up to his brother. "You want a game, Lenny?"

"No. I'm good."

Roche slid the cue into the rack. Finger laid his cue on the table and began to rack the balls.

"So what do you think, Lenny?"

"I think you shouldn't talk about that stuff. It's hard on you."

"That stuff? It's not stuff, Lenny. It's life and death. It's real and it has to be talked about. It's as much a part of human nature as screwing. But listen, Lenny, you know what I mean. What about Timmy Furtado? What do you think of that?"

"Well, I been thinking. It's probably not the usual suspects you should be thinking about. Somebody new to town, new to the 'business' world."

"You mean like Warden?"

"Yeah, like him, but not him. I got his gun, remember?"

Roche smiled at Finger and said, "Don't act like you didn't know that." Then to Lenny, "He could have gotten another gun. Or maybe Timmy had a gun and Warden used that."

Lenny raised his arms, palms up. "There you go."

Finger tightened the rack. "There is somebody new in town and they're selling coke. Timmy was selling without a vendor permit from the new people. This is what I hear."

Roche said, "OK, OK, Finger. What are you telling me?"

"If I told you what I wasn't telling you, that would be telling. And I'd tell you if I thought you were serious about not knowing." Finger looked sideways at Roche, then reached over the pool table and nudged the hanging light. It swayed and made the shadows on the floor move toward and away from Finger. "You should just do your job the best you can like you always do, Roche. You're not the mayor or the chief of police, you know."

"Yeah, and you're not my mother, Finger." Roche also gave the light over the pool table a nudge.

Finger went to a cabinet on the wall and pulled out a bottle of bourbon and three glasses. He turned and carried them to the card table and sat down with The Roach. He said, "Everybody's been asked to…do some new business, Theo."

"So why haven't I heard this?"

"Greed, mostly. Nobody wants to share with guys like you, Detective. Or maybe they figure you wouldn't take money on this one, you being opposed to drug dealing and all. So listen, they make some kind of sense. What if Lenny here is correct? Somebody unprofessional is moving drugs in our town. And you get conflict and muscle and murders. It's going to happen, with or without my friends on the Hill. So if the family controls the drug trade in our town, that makes it easy for the police to regulate hard drugs. Keep it to a minimum, so to speak, and without any unpleasant rivalries."

Roche, still standing, said, "I'm not sure I like this idea."

"That's why nobody wanted you to hear about it."

Roche said, "It ain't like betting on the dogs, for Christ's sake. It ain't like no harm no foul. We're talking hard drugs. We're talking big-time addiction here. That shit ruins lives!"

Finger opened the bottle of bourbon. "I know, I know."

"Yeah, Finger. Sorry. I don't have to tell you," Roche said, remembering that Finger's wife had died of a heroin overdose six years ago. "It stinks all the same. I can't see it for anything but an excuse to make money. You say, 'Oh well, there're going to be drug dealers anyway. Better the drug dealers are your friends'."

Lenny said, "So well put, brother Theo."

"So I'm just a pawn here, Finger?"

"No, Roche. No way. You got a say in the matter."

"Well, why didn't anybody ask? Was anybody ever gonna ask?"

"Afraid you'd say no, Roche."

"Everybody knows me here."

Finger poured himself some more bourbon and said, "Well, they don't."

"They talk to me plenty when there's a mess. They talk to me then."

Finger said, "It's always that way. The aristocrats and the peasants."

"Well, I say no. It's not because I'm all high and mighty. It's 'cause I know it won't work. It won't work 'cause it's based on greed. Based on letting people hurt themselves and making them pay money to do it. There is nothing good going to come of this. Nothing at all."

Finger said, "You're right. I just...I don't think we can fight it. My people can't. We'd be replaced in a week. They don't even have to get tough. Well...shit...maybe. One of us could take a fall."

Lenny said, "Maybe we could get help from the Feds." Both men looked at Lenny like he had two heads. "Hey, what? The Feds is all right guys. And girls, for that matter."

"What do you know about the FBI?"

"Not those Feds. The other Feds."

"What other Feds?"

"The DEA. You know Twyla? She works in a DEA office in Fall River."

"No shit? What's your big plan, Lenny?" Finger asked.

Lenny looked at his brother, then back at Finger. "I ain't got a plan. I'm just saying they might help out if they had no choice. I mean, we're nothing compared to the money the drugs bring in, but it can ruin the neighborhood. My big brother's right, Finger." Lenny shifted in his chair and continued. "I'm not saying we should fight Patriarca, but don't kid yourselves. If you play ball and all, for the good of the neighborhood, you'll eventually be sorry you did. It'll change people. Your friends will change. So think about the DEA and the ATF. If we tipped off the right people there, they would go after the bad guys for us."

Finger poured bourbon in a glass, slid it over to Lenny and said, "You're smarter than you look, Lenny."

"Yeah, I'm better lookin' than this, too."

Roche pulled a chair up to the card table and dropped into it. Finger poured him a glass of bourbon. All three examined the amber elixir, swirling it, looking for answers. Lenny spoke.

"Or… somebody could just kill the bad guys."

Neither Finger nor Theo looked up. Lenny continued, "Thing is, somebody's got to say who the bad guys are, then somebody has to do the killin'. If those two somebodies are the same person, it lets a lot of people off the hook." Lenny tossed down his bourbon and pushed himself away from the table. As he stood, he said, "That's always the thing."

The Roach placed his empty glass at the exact center of the table and walked out of Finger's basement.

Intimate Strangers

Thursday, August 29th, 1984: Fairhaven, Massachusetts

"It stinks in here," Sarah said. She hadn't found a cleaning crew she trusted, so Tom was mopping the floor when she came in after her morning run.

Tom stopped mopping. "It's a waterfront bar." Sarah continued on her way to the office in the back. Tom leaned on the mop and said, "Good morning."

Sarah pivoted toward Tom as she pushed through the double doors to the kitchen and said, "Good morning." The doors swung closed behind her.

Tom looked around the empty bar, noting how different it felt from last night at closing. His new job was to clear the cash registers and lock up the Blue Oyster at closing time. He left the mop standing in the bucket, opened the fire exit door, then propped open the front door. The perfume of fish, diesel fuel, and salt air from the wharfs mixed with the stale beer and Murphy's oil soap in the empty bar. He finished mopping, then cleaned behind the bar. He would clean the beer coolers tomorrow. After setting the chairs down off the tables, he went back to see how Sarah was doing.

When he opened the office door, she said, "Hey, Mr. Maintenance Man, open the back door please." The back door was next to the office. He pushed the bar and swung the steel door open, stepped outside, flipping the doorstop down. The hydraulic whine and banging of a garbage truck emptying a dumpster signaled that the day had officially begun. He leaned back against the door frame and lit a cigarette. He could hear Sarah on the phone with a liquor distributor. She must have known the person on the phone because the call turned into one of those *Do you remember when* conversations. She made no effort to include or exclude him in the part of her life made up of old and new friends. Whenever he heard her talk to her friends, he listened for the stories between the words. Even though she invited him into that private world from time to time, he understood it was by invitation only.

Tom heard the sound of a file cabinet drawer opening and closing. He knocked the fire off his Marlboro and tossed the butt into the dumpster, then went back inside. When he entered the office, Sarah looked up.

"Did you know one of your bartenders is dealing coke? She's hiding ten dollar hits in matchbooks."

Sarah stopped writing in her appointment book. "How do you know?"

"I saw it happen while I was putting up the new fire extinguishers yesterday. A fisherman asked for a pack of matches. I think he said waterproof matches. Yeah. Well, there was a tray of book matches on top of the bar, but Stacy reached under the bar for one and handed it to him. He took it with his right hand and left a ten dollar bill on the bar with his left." Tom walked around the desk and waited next to Sarah. She folded her arms, but didn't look up. "Who are you going to get to take numbers here, Sarah?"

"I don't know."

"It's a little too obvious for you to be doing it, don't you think?"

"Yes...."

"Yes what?"

Sarah sat up in her chair and tilted her head toward Tom. "Why don't you get a nice Quaker girlfriend and you wouldn't have to worry about these things."

"I don't deserve a nice girlfriend."

Sarah turned back to her desk and opened the leather satchel she used as a briefcase. Her hands shook as she placed the appointment book inside. She stood up but kept her head down as she stepped past him.

"I didn't mean it like that, Sarah."

She kept walking. He followed her as far as the kitchen and stopped.

Even though that's not what he meant to say Tom felt the truth in his words. He was also reminded of how he felt when he shot someone in Vietnam and wanted to take it back. Sarah went out the door. Tom stood in the middle of the kitchen, alone except for his thoughts. *More collateral damage, nowhere to hide, nowhere to run, no safe options, just survive a few more seconds then a few more minutes then....*

He closed the back door, gathered up his tools, put them in his toolbox, and left through the front. He locked the door behind him and walked toward his pickup. His pace was steady. About ten feet from the pickup, he raised the twenty-pound toolbox over his right shoulder like a shot-put, and heaved it toward the pickup bed. It bounced off the tailgate. Tom rushed up to it, picked it up, raised it over his head, then slammed it down in the pickup bed. He took a half step back and eased his way around the truck to the driver's side door. He was panting, but his motions were even and methodical. He unlocked his pickup, got in and lit a cigarette. After a deep drag he put the keys in the ignition, clicking it once. He turned on the radio. Jimi Hendrix was singing *Voodoo Child.* He turned up the volume and stared at the dashboard.

The song did not remind him of Woodstock and the Summer of Love. It brought images of sandbags, a 155 mm howitzer and concertina wire. Images of young men in jungle fatigues leaning against bunkers or crouched in the dust. He saw himself there, back on a firebase in Vietnam, standing with rifle in hand, watching a little black-and-white television. The television was perched on an ammo box against the fire control bunker for the 155 mm howitzers. Images from man's first moon landing were replaying on the screen.

A silent plea filled him,
Make it stop.
He heard the imaginary TV,
"That's one small step for man"…
He heard the radio in the bunker,
"Red Leg This Is Tiger Alpha Three."
Fire Mission!"…
And the TV,
"and one giant leap for mankind"…
And the radio,
"Three Rounds H.E. Airburst! Fire For
Effect!"

His silent plea became a prayer,
Make It Stop.
He felt the muzzle blast from the howitzer,
Make it STOP.
He saw shrapnel tear vegetation and flesh with equal efficiency,
Make IT STOP.
He could smell cordite, diesel fuel,
burning excrement,
MAKE IT STOP!

It did not stop, only receded. The voice in his head became a snuffing predator, waiting, watching, knowing its prey had no escape.

The Mark of Cain

Monday, September 2nd, 1984: Fairhaven, Massachusetts

The deserted beach at night felt safer to Tom than a Sunday morning sidewalk. There was no moon that night, so he used his flashlight as he made his way back from the beach through the salt marsh. He switched off the flashlight as he left the path and stepped onto the street two blocks from Sarah's house. The lights in Fairhaven reflected off the overcast sky enough for Tom to make out the edge of the street where the blacktop contrasted with the sand and grass.

Tom approached the house and noted a car across the street parked next to the empty lot and saw Sarah's car was not in the driveway. He felt disappointed, then relieved, then apprehensive. The front door was ajar. The only light came from the hallway. Tom edged around the side of the house and peered in through the large windows, which faced the beach. Detective Roche was sitting at the dining room table. Tom went back to the front door, walked through, pulling it closed behind him.

Without looking up, Detective Roche said, "We need to talk, Tom."

"Now? You want to talk now?"

"Now would be best."

Tom raised his arms, then let them drop "Well then, I guess we'll talk." Tom flipped on a light, walked over, and sat sideways opposite Roche. "How did you get in?"

Detective Roche leaned in and rested his elbows on the table. "I wasn't always a detective."

He slid his hand into the inside pocket of his leather jacket and produced a pack of Marlboros, took one and flipped the pack across the table to Tom. Tom slipped a cigarette from the pack and placed it between his lips. He eyed the detective, got up and walked around the breakfast counter into the kitchen area. He got a bottle opener from a drawer and two Heinekens from the fridge. He sat back down, set a beer in front of Roche, opened one for himself and scooted the opener across the table to the detective. Roche sat back in his chair and opened the beer. They lit their cigarettes, took long drags and exhaled.

Detective Roche placed his cigarette in the ashtray between them. "Did you kill Timmy Furtado?"

"No…no way."

"I need to be sure of that, Tom."

"I didn't kill Timmy. OK?"

Detective Roche shoved his chair back and stood. His grey eyes held Tom's. Leaning in, he said, "You sure as fuck killed somebody. You're guilty. I can feel it. Why *is* that?" He straightened and put his hands on his hips. "If you don't tell me the truth I will hound you for the rest of your days and into whatever comes after. Tell me, or I - will - own - your - life."

Detective Roche eased himself back down into the chair and folded his arms across his chest. Tom looked at the mirror hanging on the wall behind Roche. He could see himself looking at Roche.

"Sarah said you were in Korea?"

"Marines."

"Officer?"

"Lieutenant."

"OCS?"

"Battlefield commission." Roche unfolded his arm and rubbed his chin. "First I was a platoon sergeant. My lieutenant took early retirement. I got his job."

Tom took a drag off his cigarette, looked at the ceiling and said, "Things must have been pretty clear-cut in Korea."

Theodore Roche reached for his cigarette, flicked ashes and took a tight frowning drag. He exhaled at the ashtray while grinding out the Marlboro down to its filter. He settled back in his chair, elbows on the armrest, fingers interlaced and said, "No, Tom, things were not clear-cut. Not even in the Korean War. Civilians are killed in every war and soldiers like you and me, men like you and me, do the killing." Tom was staring at the table. Detective Roche pressed on. "Remember the story in the Bible about Cain and Abel? It's the first documented murder in human history. Cain killed his brother Abel and God gave Cain an indelible mark. You have that mark, Tom. Do you want to tell me about it?"

"No."

Roche nodded once and said, "The memories just keep pushing, Tom. The stories just keep telling themselves over and over and over again in your head until you let them out."

Tom looked at Roche, then his eyes lost focus as he turned away and looked at the corner of the table. He remembered the sulfur smell of a smoke grenade, the weight of his backpack, the feel of a rifle in his hand. He took on the appearance of a crouched predator. He didn't like the feeling itself, but he liked the power of it. He didn't want the memories, but he knew Detective Roche was right. They just kept coming without warning. He didn't know why one particular story showed up instead of another.

Tom was motionless. He searched the other man's face, found his eyes. Those gray eyes did not hold compassion or judgment, but a vastness waiting for the truth to flow in. The timeless bond between Tom Warden and Theodore Roche was deeper than any lovers could have. It was born of a primal intimacy shared by men who hunted and killed other men.

Tom let his tenuous grip on the present slip, and Sgt. Warden began to speak.

> It was the spring of 1969. We had chased some VC into a village. The village was supposed to be empty. We were searching hooches. Guy in first platoon got shot in the face poking his head into a bunker built inside one of the hooches. A lot of 'em had small mud shelters inside like that so they could protect themselves from whichever side was shooting up the village, but the guy in first platoon—Redman, I think got blown away when he went inside one of the hooches, so we started tossing grenades into the hooches before we went in.
>
> I was getting up to move when I caught movement on my left. I spun and shot a man coming

> at me. I hit him with a short burst. Stopped his forward momentum; straightened him up. He dropped to his knees, hands still over his head. He died on his knees and flopped face down in front of me. I stepped around the old man I had just shot to death and went into the hut. When my eyes adjusted to the darkness, I saw an old woman lying near the back of the hooch. I knelt beside her. She was trying to speak. I shook my head. She pushed the blanket down off her chest. I pulled it the rest of the way back and saw two stumps where her legs should have been. I dropped the blanket and crawled from the hut. I squatted back on my heels beside the dead man. Shark, my point man, walked up to the old man in front of me and slipped an AK-47 under the body's right arm, then bent down to me and said, Fuck it…It don't mean nuthin'. The body count was three VC. That included the man I had killed who was only trying to protect the only family he had left.

Tom remained motionless as he stared past Roche. Detective Roche looked over his right shoulder at the mirror hanging on the wall behind him, then back at Tom. "I know remembering that was hard, son. I know telling it was even harder. It won't be the last time you have to do it, so you might as well get used to it. You have to admit to what you did, what you became if you ever want to be anything different. You have to tell your story. Then you can come home."

Tom stood. "I didn't kill Timmy."

"I believe you."

A car pulled into the driveway. Tom picked up the ashtray, took it to the bathroom, dumped the ashes in the toilet, and washed out the ashtray with soap and water. When he came back out to the front room, Sarah came in. Roche stood and acknowledged her.

She said, “Hi, Theo. How ya doin’?”

“OK, I guess.”

Sarah looked at the ashtray in Tom’s hands. She left the front door open and walked across the room and threw open a window. “You guys been smoking.”

Roche gathered the beer bottles from the table and said, “Sorry about that, Sarah. We got to talking and I lit up.”

Sarah extended her hand toward the ashtray Tom was still holding and said, “I’ll take that.” Tom handed her the ashtray. She took it out to the front porch.

Roche stepped toward the front door and turned back to Tom. “Remember what I said, Tom; and don’t leave town just yet, either.” Tom nodded and Roche walked out the open front door.

* * *

Sarah was waiting in the driveway. “Is he going to be OK, Theo?”

“I don’t know, Sarah. How about you? You going to be OK?”

“Maybe. I’m not OK now, though.” She folded her arms and looked at the ground. “I know he loves me and I love him, but it doesn’t seem to make any difference. I feel cheated. Love is supposed to feel good, but it just hurts. The closer we get, the more it hurts." She bit her upper lip. Theo couldn't see them, but he knew there were tears. He started to reach out. Sarah inched back, turned a shoulder to him and looked out toward the ocean.

"I'm sorry," he said, "There is no fixing this, Sarah. Try to trust that something better will come." Sarah scraped the ground with her toe, turned, and walked back to the house. Theo watched a long shadow follow her through the door, then she closed it behind her.

* * *

Roche got in his car and drove across the causeway back into Fairhaven.

When Sarah came in, Tom was standing with his hands on the breakfast counter looking at the floor. She walked past him down the hallway and into the bedroom. He went and lay down on the couch that separated the dining area from the living area. It was midnight.

Blood Trail

Saturday, September 7th, 1984: Fairhaven, Massachusetts

"Order up," The Roach said as he placed the bowl of kale soup at the end of the stainless steel counter. Louise stopped rolling silverware into napkins, picked up the steaming bowl and took it out to the waiting customer. It was nine o'clock. The Ferry Café kitchen was now closed.

Mel, the busboy, pushed through the kitchen doors with a tray of dirty dishes. He was only twenty-three, but he walked hunched slightly forward like an old lady. He set the tray down, adjusted his thick-lensed glasses with both hands. "You want me to wash the dishes now, Lenny?"

"Yes, Mel, wash the dishes now. It's time to close the kitchen."

"OK, Lenny, I'll wash the dishes now." Mel had worked in the kitchen with The Roach for six years, but he looked around the kitchen, holding his glasses securely in place with both hands, until he found the sink. He walked to it and began washing dishes with the reverence of a priest saying Mass. Lenny put the last of the kale soup in a to-go container. He placed the container, along with some dinner rolls and clam cakes, into a brown paper grocery bag, then continued to get his kitchen ready for the next day.

Andrea, the gum-chewing, fast-talking, red headed single mom night-shift waitress, bubbled through the kitchen doors. When she passed Mel she said, "Hello, handsome."

"Hi, An Dee," Mel said without looking up. Andrea went over to Lenny and handed him a copy of JD Salinger's play, *A Lie of the Mind.*

Lenny said, "Did you like it, Andy?"

"Not really. There was no happy ending. Too much like real life," she said over her shoulder.

Lenny picked up the grocery bag with his free hand. "Andy…here's something for the kids."

She turned, came back to him, and accepted the bag. "Thanks, Lenny. You're a prince." Mel's determined motions had stopped. He stood at the sink with both hands in the soapy water.

Lenny said, "Just keep washing the dishes Mel." Mel resumed his cleansing of dishes and utensils. By ten, the kitchen was ready for the next day. Mel said good night and went out. Lenny went out through the back door and up the open stairway to his rooms above the Ferry Café.

While he showered, Lenny The Roach thought about his plan. He thought the two men who had visited Sarah at the Blue Oyster would be the perfect pair to frame for Timmy's murder. If he left the .45 he had used to kill Timmy on one of their bodies it would tie everything up with a pretty bow. It would look like the new muscle in town had been sending a message and got a message in return. The message part was true and Lenny knew a little truth made the big lie believable.

He liked the idea of a message from The Roach, the recycler of the unclean. He understood people would accept a simple lie before a less palatable and more complex picture of reality, especially if that lie kept them separated from the dark side of humanity. He didn't see his killing as any different from an execution by the state or a soldier's sanctioned killing. He understood that, whether done by a mob, a government, a gang or an individual, killing another human being was a very personal thing...and he liked doing it. He understood most people were content to let someone like him do the killing for them.

After showering, he gave himself a clean shave, brushed and flossed his teeth. He dressed himself in khaki slacks and a wool crewneck sweater, put on his navy blue pea coat and left for Big Dan's in New Bedford's north end, where he would meet Arthur. Arthur Borden, aka Butter Bean, was the guy you went to if you wanted to buy or sell a hundred or so pounds of pot.

Lenny went into Big Dan's and scanned the bar for Butter Bean. He saw him sitting with someone at a table in the back corner so he took a seat at the end of the bar facing the front door and ordered a beer. A few minutes later, he saw the man that had been sitting with Butter Bean, leave the bar. Lenny took his beer and walked back to the table in the rear. Butter Bean moved a basket of peanuts aside. Lenny set his beer in the space provided and sat down. "How ya doin', Bean?"

"All is well, Roach, all is well."

"Is the import business still good for you?"

"It's smooth, real smooth. Not like when you and I were doing it. No more rowboats in the salt marshes. I just set up the situation and handle the money now.

That's mostly what I did for you tonight. I set up the deal with the two guys you wanted, but I won't…"

The waitress approached and set a steaming bowl of butter beans with chorizo in front of Arthur. She looked at the two men looking back at her and left the table. "I won't handle the money on this one, though." He picked up a soupspoon, stirred his beans once and looked up at Lenny. "I don't want to be connected to any hard drugs, so I did like you said and covered myself. I told them to watch their backs; I wasn't making any guarantees. OK, Lenny?"

"That's good." The Roach took a swallow of beer. "So what's the deal?"

"Meet at Destruction Brook Woods trailhead off Slades Corner Road; two am." Butter Bean took a spoonful and chewed. "Maybe I should retire and become a movie star."

"What?"

"A movie star. They put me in a Budweiser commercial, ya know? I get residuals."

Lenny laughed. "Butter Bean on the big screen. I can see that." He stood, and placed his chair against the table. "Thanks Arthur."

Arthur nodded and went back to his beans and chorizo. The Roach turned and left Big Dan's. He drove in his station wagon to Russells Mills Road and followed it to Horseneck Road, then right on Slades Corner Road. He drove a quarter-mile past the trailhead on the deserted road, parked and checked the dashboard clock. *Plenty of time*. He doused the headlights and killed the engine.

The pay phone on the wall in the back of Big Dan's rang. Butter Bean reached back over his right shoulder, lifted the receiver and spoke into it. "Yeah?" he said, then listened. He switched the receiver to his left, and turned toward the wall. "It's all set; and like I said, he's paying for it himself." He hung up the phone.

At 1:30 a.m. The Roach got out of the station wagon and opened the rear hatch. He lifted the spare tire cover and retrieved Timmy Furtado's .45 auto in the shoulder holster and a .25 caliber automatic, which he took back to the front seat with him. He put on the shoulder holster with Timmy's .45, being careful not to touch the weapon. He put his pea coat back on and slipped the .25 auto into the left pocket. He drove back the quarter mile, turned down the wooded lane leading back to the trailhead. He parked the station wagon fifty feet from Destruction Brook Creek, and waited.

At 2:10 a.m., he saw headlights through the trees. The approaching car slowed as it neared the turnoff. He turned on his headlights, counted to three, and shut them off. The dark-colored four-door sedan rolled to a stop just off the left front bumper of the station wagon. The Roach took the keys from the ignition, eased the driver's side door open and got out. He walked around the door and stood by the front fender.

The dome light in the station wagon presented his silhouette to the other vehicle. Two men got out. The driver wore slacks, a crew-neck sweater, and a London Fog topcoat. The passenger wore jeans, flannel shirt and a watch cap. The man in the London Fog approached Lenny. The man in the watch cap raised his weapon, a

.38 special, then walked over and stood behind Lenny The Roach. The topcoat man stepped forward and said, "I'm going to pat you down." The Roach raised his arms slightly, allowing the man to frisk him.

The man felt the .45 immediately. He opened The Roach's coat and pulled it from the shoulder holster. "What have we here?" He thumbed the hammer back and held it at waist level. He reached out with his left hand, and turned The Roach by the shoulder toward the station wagon. "Just put your hands on the hood for me." He stepped to his left and motioned with the .45. "See if he has anything else."

The man in the watch cap holstered his weapon and began to pat down The Roach, starting with his ankles and working up. He found the 25 auto in The Roach's left coat pocket and took it out.

He stepped back and said, " That's it."

"Where's the money?" the man in the topcoat asked.

"Backseat," The Roach said.

"Get it."

The Roach tightened his grip on the ignition key, got his feet under him, straightened, and began turning to his left. Driving hard with his legs, The Roach swung his right arm around and stabbed the man wearing the watch cap in the eye with the ignition key. The man in the topcoat raised Timmy's .45 automatic. The Roach snatched the 25-caliber auto from the other man's hand as it came up in a defensive gesture.

The man in the topcoat pulled the trigger. The hammer fell on an empty chamber. The Roach shot him in the throat. The bullet went through the soft tissue into his spine and he slumped to the ground. The Roach grabbed the man in the watch cap by the shoulder. Placing the pistol under his ear, he put a bullet into his brain stem. As the man fell away The Roach took the watch cap from the man's head and used it to wipe the fingerprints from the .25 automatic. He sent the watch cap and pistol in a high arc towards Destruction Brook. When he heard the splash, The Roach turned, got in his station wagon and went home.

Claymore

June 1969: Republic of South Vietnam

Alpha Company was on a company-sized operation looking for Charlie. Sgt. Warden had been in country six months and had taken on the grim determination of a combat veteran. No longer terrified of death, and so able to go about the business of soldiering as if it was the only thing he'd ever done or ever would do. The rifle company moved out from the LZ in three columns into the bush. Warden's squad had point for second platoon. The brush was thick and full of what the grunts called wait-a-minute vines. The thorns hooked into jungle fatigues and skin. The CO was pushing them hard so the men couldn't stop to untangle themselves. They just ripped through. They all knew the captain and lieutenants were just as cut up by the vines and they shouldn't complain, but they did anyway. Someone would just blurt out, "Fucking brass." Even so, when Lt. Stark got a bunch of fire ants down his neck, two of his men helped him strip his gear and brush the ants off his back. Just like in any war, these men lived and died together.

After about an hour of humping, Alpha Company came to an area where the bamboo was so thick the only way through was single file on a footpath. This was exactly what they always tried to avoid, but there was no other place to walk. If the VC ambushed them in there, everybody would be blown away.

Sgt. Warden felt a queasiness in his stomach. It was beyond the danger he felt from the situation of being strung out, single file, in a bamboo thicket. It used to feel strange, but now he knew the suggestion of a purple haze clinging to the edges of his sight meant someone was going to die. He could tell some of the greener troops were glad to be on a footpath instead of the brush, and were starting to relax. He let Woody pass him and said, just loud enough to be heard by the rest of his squad, "Keep it spread out, OK? Just stay alert...and quiet." Warden turned back up the trail. When he caught up to Woody, he reached out and turned the volume down on the squad radio so Woody could barely hear it. The typical banter of soldiers on patrol faded away as each man became aware that all his hopes and dreams could vanish in a violent, painful, solitary death.

Alpha Company came to an open area and fanned out into a perimeter of sorts. It was about noon, so they broke out lunch rations and ate. There were enough trees to get some shade and that made it a good break. They all relaxed a little. The tension built up in the bamboo thicket eased. The purple haze of death went back to the place it always waited in Sgt. Warden's mind as he surveyed his men. The two new guys in his squad sat together. They were more nervous than scared. The old-timers, who had learned what there was to be afraid of, were *never* nervous, just scared.

It was time to move out. Sgt. Warden shouldered into his rucksack and spoke to his squad. "We're going to move in a few minutes." He walked over to the two new guys, who were both leaning against the same small tree and talking. "Stop talking and finish your chow. We're moving out soon." Warden stepped between the new guys and another small tree to go up and check with Johnson, his point man. He asked him about the terrain up ahead. Johnson said he thought there might be some tunnels. They were near a deep gully, and Johnson pointed out some openings in the bank.

The purple haze was back. They were at the edge of a tunnel complex. There were probably some bunkers and spider holes. Woody had turned the volume back up, so Sgt. Warden heard the call on the radio to saddle-up. As he approached his squad he saw they were already up and starting to bunch together, shooting the shit. Warden knew it felt more secure for them in a group, but was thinking of the tunnels. He said, "Spread the fuck out," and told the new guys to move up to the point man, who was about sixty feet away.

Sgt. Warden was standing about fifteen feet from the two new guys when they got up and walked between the same two trees he had. He turned away from them and the ground behind him exploded. The next thing Warden was aware of was being facedown in dried leaves, and wondering why it was so quiet. Then he was standing, looking at a cloud of dust where the two new guys had been. Nobody moved. He just stood there, thinking there was something he should be doing. Red, the platoon medic, ran up. Sgt. Warden couldn't see the rest of his squad. *Where the fuck are my guys?* He barely heard Lt. Stark shouting into the radio.

Sgt. Warden shuffled toward the spot where the new guys were supposed to be. He saw Phil pop up and swing the M-60 machine gun toward the right flank, and lay down behind it. Then Rawlings stuck his head up and yelled. "Sarge, you OK?"

Warden yelled back, "Yeah."

To Warden it sounded like he was in a shower room. Then his adrenaline kicked in. He patted himself down, looking for tears in his fatigues or blood soaked spots. The company medic had come up. He and Red were both working on someone. *Fuck, I got three guys missing.* He picked his way the last ten feet back to where the two new guys had been. There was a small crater near the tree they had rested against. He walked around the little trees where Red and Jack were working on one of the new guys. He walked a few steps and saw the other new guy, arms and legs spread out and bleeding from small black holes in his forehead and cheeks.

Villalobos was checking his pulse. He looked up at Sgt. Warden and said. "This one's still alive." About five feet behind him, Warden saw Donald lying on his back, his hands covering his face. Warden yelled, "Don…Don!"

Donald propped himself up on one elbow and dropped back flat. Warden rushed over to him. He was still breathing and tried to push him away. *Just a concussion, he will live.*

Third squad's medic had come up. Villalobos got up and made room for the medic. He walked out twenty feet to the right front and squatted behind a tree. He waved at Phil to make sure the machine-gunner knew he was over there. Phil smiled, gave him the finger and looked back into the brush. Sgt. Warden got Donald to sit up. He checked again for blood but didn't find any. He tried to talk to Donald, but Donald wouldn't answer. He just stared straight ahead. Somebody popped smoke and in less than a minute, he heard a chopper. First platoon had secured the LZ on their left flank.

Sgt. Warden had four men left out of seven. They secured the right flank. Third squad had lined up on the gully where the tunnels were. The men from first squad loaded the three casualties onto the medevac chopper. One head wound, one with hamburger where his upper thighs used to be, and Donald, who sat bolt upright on the stretcher. Donald had the perfect thousand-yard stare.

Warden watched the medevac helicopter leave, then started thinking about the wound pattern on the new guy's head and where he last saw him walking. Before the booby trap was triggered, they were still bunched up. He went to the spot where the small crater was. He figured it must have been a claymore mine, judging from the perfectly round holes in the new guy's head and face. A claymore mine was made up of a layer of C-4 explosive on the backside, and seven hundred steel balls on the front face. The first man got hit high in the thighs, the second in the face, the third only by dirt and shockwave.

He took his bayonet out and poked around the hole left by the explosion and found a pair of wires. He pulled gently, bit by bit, looking for another booby trap. The wires led to a canvas bag made specifically for the claymore mines they carried. Inside was a discarded radio battery. Another pair of wires led to the middle of the footpath between the two trees that the point man, Warden, and the two new guys had walked between. At the end of the wires he found a small plastic insect repellent bottle, just like the ones they carried. The plastic bottle and the lid from a C-ration can had been fashioned into a pressure switch, and buried just beneath the surface.

Johnson and Sgt. Warden had walked over it. The new guy walking third stepped on the trigger and got his legs blown off. He died three days later. The new guy walking fourth died in the chopper. They had been in Nam less than a month. They had come to Sgt. Warden's squad just two weeks ago. Donald, who walked fifth, never returned to the field. Sgt. Warden remembered Donald used to walk point and thought he probably felt fairly safe that day walking fifth.

Sgt. Thomas Warden got a small waterproof pouch from his rucksack and sat down. He opened the pouch, removed a 3 x 5 notebook, and opened it to a list of names. He found Donald's name and circled it. The names of his two new men were together at the bottom. Without reading them, he put a line through each.

Hiding the Soul

Saturday, September 14th, 1984: Fairhaven, Massachusetts

Tom and Sarah had followed a path through the trees and salt marshes to the far side of West Island where there was an isolated beach. Usually they didn't talk much. They would just be together on the beach. Sarah pushed her hands deeper into the pockets of her insulated vest and spoke more to the ocean than to Tom. "When I asked my father why mom killed herself, he said, 'She ran out of options'. I like to keep my options open. Dad fell asleep on the couch in his den that night. The next morning, when he went upstairs to their bedroom, he found Mom. I guess she took a bottle of sleeping pills and never woke up. Didn't leave a note. I was sixteen."

They stood, watching the ocean. Tom said, "I kind of know what he meant—about running out of options. You never know for sure, though." They started to make their way back along the beach the way they had come.

Sarah looked over at Tom. "So, what about you? Are you thinking about options?" Tom didn't answer. He slowed his pace and walked half a step behind Sarah. She turned toward him, stopping and said, "You *do* think about options don't you? You know, hopes and dreams?"

Tom stopped, stepped past her and looked away. He took a deep breath. "Sometimes I feel like I have no place. Not that I don't know where my place is, but that there is actually no place for me, no purpose. I feel in the end it will have made no difference that I ever lived at all."

"That's grim. Just how much difference would you have to make in order to feel better?"

"I never thought of that."

Sarah smiled. "You could clean the garage. That would make a difference."

"I'm serious."

"So am I. How can you be sure you haven't made a difference?"

"Well, I'm talking about a consistent direction. Not random living. Even the life of a cow has a pattern. You can see they take the same trails. You can see where the herd has grazed."

"You're talking about cows now? Is that how it is with you? You feel like a lone cow unable to fit in with the herd?"

"Actually, I picture myself as a lone wolf. Maybe that's what's depressing me, making me feel desperate."

"Yes, I suppose a lone cow trying to fit into a wolf pack might feel desperate. Anyway, you think too much. You get way out there sometimes."

"You're the one talking about a cow wanting to be a wolf."

"Yes, and you're the one trying to figure out what that would be like. You're not a cow, Tom, or a lone wolf. You're a man with a garage full of junk and trash. If you want to make a difference, clean the garage. I'm serious. Clean the garage without trying to fit that into the meaning of life."

"Yeah, maybe. But I'll just fill it with trash again. What's the use?"

"That's about the way I feel when I talk to *you*, Tom. What's the use. No matter how much encouragement I give, you can always find the dark side!"

"When we talk about you and *your* despair, I always find a bright side, or some hope at least. That's what makes me feel desperate. Hopeless and desperate. Most of the time when I bring up myself or my concerns, the person I'm talking to will turn the conversation back to themselves in the very next sentence. It's no wonder I talk to myself. I'm the only one who will listen."

"Maybe you're talking to the wrong people."

"I'm talking to the people I care about. I'm talking to the people that care about me. And it always ends the same way—talking about their hopes and dreams, what they fear, what they love—never about me. These are the people who say they love me. You say you love me and I know you do, but ninety percent of the conversations we have are about you, your family, your goals. Maybe I should change the company I keep."

Sarah stopped and folded her arms across her chest.

Tom continued. "I have a life of quiet desperation and I'm surrounded by people with lives of shouting desperation."

Sarah stopped and put her hands on her hips. "God *damn* it." Tom stopped and put his hands in his pockets. She continued, "Stop making this my fault. Don't say I never listen to you when you talk about yourself because you *never* talk about yourself. You crack a joke and change the subject if we start to talk about you. When you get in one of your moods, you ignore me. If I try to find out what's bothering you, you disappear for a day or two. Like right now—you're looking at the sand, not at me." Tom turned around and looked at the sand at Sarah's feet. She loosened her arms and rubbed her palms together. "You do help me. You seem to understand and really care about me, but maybe it's not a good thing for you to be around me. You don't clean the garage because you need time to think about your own life. I clean the garage so I don't have to think about my own life."

"So what should we do, Sarah?"

"I don't know what we should do, but maybe you should find a hot babe who doesn't think too much, but likes to clean the garage! Ha!" She threw her head back and laughed, pleased with the picture she painted .

"Yes, but what would me and this babe talk about?"

"I said hot babe, not dumb broad. You'll find something to talk about after the garage gets cleaned."

And there it was. Sarah had jokingly, but seriously, proposed a solution for Tom. They were both trying to make sense of their lives, but that did not mean they could do it in the same way. Tom knew the solution for him was not what she wanted, but what she thought would work for him. He knew her heart. He could always see to the core of someone else, but not himself.

Tom did not want to leave her, but thought she would probably be better off with a man who could clean the garage after a fulfilling day at his life's work, just because the garage needed cleaning. Someone to be an example of the way she could be her best. He wanted desperately for her dreams to come true and would do almost anything to help her, but he couldn't even help himself. He had no dreams. He had given them all up. Now he was living someone else's dream. It was wrong for her. It was wrong for him.

He knew he'd have to leave. He wouldn't leave her for another woman. It felt like that to him, though. The other woman was the Vietnam War. He could no longer ask for her intimacy when he withheld his own. The black rage building inside him was getting harder to control, and he was afraid one day he would hurt her. None of this was clear in Tom Warden's unquiet mind. The only thing he was sure of is that he wanted a decent interval before he actually left. A slow separation, so the gap would fill easily behind them. He had, unknowingly, started the separation months ago—the holding back, the hiding, and he was already starting to hurt.

They finished their walk in silence.

Death Ground

July 1969: Republic of South Vietnam

Sgt. Warden was getting his squad ready to go out on ambush. Second squad would take trucks from the forward firebase near Binh Canh to a drop-off point, then walk out into the rice paddies. Warden sensed a change in the radio chatter coming from the CP. When Lieutenant Stewart got back from the CP, he told his squad leaders there was VC activity in a nearby village and that Alpha Company had gotten the call to cordon off the village. No name, just a little village. It was easier when you didn't know names.

Sgt. Warden's level of fear, always there in a combat zone, ticked up. Any change in plans increased the possibility of a cluster fuck. Lt. Stewart had been in country two weeks. This would be his first field experience. Another tick of fear. The idea of executing a plan with military precision is a myth. There wasn't much time. Alpha Company had to get to the village before Charlie could *di di mau.* They were in a hurry in a combat zone. Another tick of fear. Lieutenant Stewart didn't even have time to get the correct maps for his squad leaders. There were no choppers available on such short notice. They would take trucks—more time lost. It would be dusk by the time they got to the village. Sgt. Warden told his men to saddle up. He knew his guys knew what to do, except for George, the FNG. George was a regular army reservist that got activated and sent to Nam. The rest of the squad were vets of at least three months. No short timers.

Alpha Company had formed up and was filing out through a gap in the concertina wire. Lt. Stewart turned back toward his men and shouted. “Let’s move it!”

Sgt. Warden didn’t hear confidence in the lieutenant’s voice. He didn’t want to make it hard for the new lieutenant. Even though Stewart was a lieutenant, he was also an FNG. Second platoon pretended to move faster, or less slowly, but really didn’t. They settled into the resigned shuffle they could sustain all day in the heat and damp. George was still nervous as hell. His eyes were intense, searching.

Warden knew George would settle down soon enough when he realized he was in a one-year marathon. It didn’t take more than a few weeks in Nam for a man to realize that he just can’t sustain that keyed-up state, and a forced dullness shields him from the threat of a violent death. They called it *The Thousand Yard Stare*. The soldiers couldn’t look inward; there was too much loneliness. They couldn’t look at what was right in front of them; it held the promise of a violent death. They looked out to a Detroit sidewalk or a dock in Galveston. In the beginning, that stare was an eternal moment of longing for the day they could go back to the world. In the end, it was the way a man dissipated himself in order to escape where and what he was.

Alpha Company was loaded onto the deuce-and-a-half trucks. Sgt. Warden spoke to himself more than his men. “Lock and load”. The *schlick-chunk* of rounds being chambered could be heard up and down the line of trucks rolling out. Warden looked at the FNG's weapon. It was on safe. George gripped his instrument of death. Warden knew the clutching hold would become a caress. Shark was sitting next to the new guy, who was hunched forward, looking at his jungle boots.

"Hey Sarge", Shark said. "Do you think we'll get a body count?"

"Who gives a fuck." Warden answered.

One corner of Shark's mouth turned up. He nudged George with his elbow and said, "You know the difference between an NVA soldier and a baby?"

"Ugh…no." George answered.

Shark said, "The NVA soldier leaves a bigger pile of charcoal." Shark's grin filled his face.

"Fuck you, Shark," Phil said. Phil was married and had a six-month-old girl. She was born a few months before he got sent to Nam. George closed his mouth and swallowed. He tried to laugh, but couldn't. Shark held his steel pot down with his left hand, leaned back, and looked ahead over the side of the deuce-and-a-half. He surveyed the rice paddies, then slumped back in the bench seat.

He laid his M-16 across his chest at port arms and said, "Fuck it. It don't mean nuthin'." Sgt. Warden adjusted his position, rolled with the motion of the truck and waited as the convoy moved closer to Can Duoc village.

It was dusk when the trucks slowed. Sgt. Warden could see the village they were going to cordon off. His platoon was in the first two trucks, which stopped just past the big dike leading into the village. The first huts of the village were about forty yards from the dirt road and the rows of hooches, on either side of the dike, stretched back another eighty yards to a line of nipa palm and brush. He figured there was a canal in that brush line, which gave Charlie easy access in and out of the village.

Sargent Braden's third squad had formed up to take point and was moving into the rice paddies, dry this time of year. Sgt. Warden, with second squad, piled out of the trucks and followed Braden's squad. The trucks carrying the company commander, first platoon, and third platoon had rolled to a stop just short of the village. Sgt. Braden moved his point squad parallel to the line of hooches, which were twenty yards to his right. Warden angled a little toward the line of hooches, closer to the small dike which was about two feet wide and a foot high. Lt. Stewart was with Sgt. Larsen and the first squad. They fell in behind second squad.

Sgt. Warden stopped and looked back to check his squad and saw they were nicely spaced and staggered. He waited for Shark and George to pass him. He had Shark walking point so he could train George, walking second. Shark liked walking point. Phil, with his round face and natural smile, waited for Woody to pass. Woody carried the squad radio and walked fourth, behind Sgt. Warden. Woody said something to Phil as he sauntered past him. Phil smiled and shouldered the M-60 machine gun, took a few steps to the right, and waited for the spacing to increase. Jefferson walked sixth. He carried the M-79 grenade launcher. Villalobos walked seventh with his M-16. Jefferson and Villalobos were a little too close together, but they were buddies and both had more time in country than anyone else in the squad. Jefferson and Villalobos watched everybody's back.

Sgt. Warden and his squad settled into the business at hand. He wouldn't have said so, but at that moment, Sgt. Warden loved his men. There was another feeling, not as close to the surface, but just as strong. At last he was Sgt. Rock, the hard man he wanted to be, ready to go into battle with his men. He loved what he was doing. He loved the power of it.

It was starting to get dark. Braden's point man was angling in toward the village, headed for the spot where the row of hooches met the brush-lined canal. Sgt. Warden looked back at the road. The trucks were long gone. The drivers would be trying to get back to a firebase before dark. He couldn't see first or third platoon. They were probably on the other side of the village with the company commander. Lt. Stewart hadn't told Sgt. Warden anything. He figured the lieutenant must have given Braden orders when they were getting off the trucks. It was getting dark fast. Braden's point was lost in shadow, but Warden knew he should be getting near the brush line. *Not good.* It was almost dark and they were still moving. *No sweat, we'll be in position behind the dike in a few minutes.* At least that's what they usually did. In daylight, usually. But lieutenant Stewart was new—really new. A week in country and this was his first night in the field. A cluster fuck in the making.

Third squad was angling in toward the west end of the village where the hooch-line met the canal. First and second squad were about ten yards from the small dike on their right. Fifteen yards beyond that, they could see the silhouette of hooches against the nearly dark sky. A few stars were starting to show themselves. Shark angled in toward the dike trying to keep the last man of the third squad in sight. George was next, walking in a crouch. Moving like a crippled elephant. Not graceful, like Phil. Warden looked back to check his guys. Woody was trailing him, as usual. He could tell it was Woody by the way his steel pot was tilted back on his head like a baseball cap, and the barely visible form of the radio he carried. Phil was next. His silhouette moved like a gazelle; a gazelle with a machine gun. After Phil there would be Jefferson. He couldn't see him, but he would be there with Villalobos.

Villalobos and Jefferson were probably too close to each other. Close enough to talk softly and still understand each other. Not so close that a burst from an AK would get them both, but close enough to be blown away by a single booby trap. Warden figured it was their choice. They felt safer being close even if they weren't. The unspoken truth was, neither wanted to survive the others death. They both carried a couple hundred rounds of linked ammo for the 60. *Business as usual.*

Charlie opened up on the point squad with an AK-47. Sgt. Warden dove for the dike between him and the village. Before he hit the baked rice paddy mud, an M-16 answered the AK. He saw Shark grab George's shoulder and pull him down and forward. Warden crawled toward the foot-high dike as a line of green tracers swept out of the hooch near the canal.

"Fuck."

He changed directions and moved toward Phil in sort of a lurch-crawl. Phil was firing into the hooches in front of him. He heard Jefferson thumping rounds into the village. Villalobos was crawling up on Phil's right, pushing a box of M-60 ammo. Warden slapped Phil's left boot and Phil released the trigger.

Warden lurched the last few feet up to the dike and yelled, "Shift fire left! See the tracers?" Phil swung the muzzle and let go a twenty round burst. "Careful! No farther left. Sgt. Braden is over there almost up to the huts."

Phil nodded once and squeezed the trigger. Warden rolled to his left to make room for Villalobos and his box of linked amo for the machine gun, then crawled along the dike to his left toward Woody and the radio. He heard George on full auto.

Warden passed Woody and yelled to George, "Conserve ammo! Single shot. One round at a time. Aim low. Fire at the muzzle flashes, just like you were trained."

George was shaking so much it was hard for him to get another magazine locked. This was his first firefight, in the dark besides. George aimed. He fired. Aimed again. Fired. The pop and crackle of small arms fire peaked. AK 47 rounds popping past at twice the speed of sound gave Warden the feeling he was in a giant popcorn machine. Woody had turned up the speaker on the prick-25. Warden could hear breaking squelch and radio traffic. He crawled up to Woody's left and looked back toward George. He couldn't help thinking of a pissed off turtle. Pissed off, determined and scared shitless.

Sgt. Warden was scared too and he was angry. He thought of Phil's six-month-old daughter, then George, so afraid to die, and Villalobos whose wife was three months pregnant. *Those rat-fucking villagers let VC into their village and now they're trying to kill us! To kill me and my guys*! Sgt. Warden called on the black rage, his willing ally. There was room for one more thought, *By God, Kerry will not raise that child alone. None of my guys will die tonight. I will not fucking die tonight*. Then the rage took him past fear to a primal state, to a need to do extreme violence, to a determination to kill anyone who stood against him. Most would say Sgt. Warden's reaction was a survival mechanism. In the end, it was merely a way of not dying.

Phil loaded another belt into his machine gun. Warden could hear the thump of an M-79 off to his right, followed by a detonation off to his left front. Zak was dropping rounds on the Chi-Com gunner. Phil gave a short burst and waited. The green tracers had stopped coming. The pop of small arms fire was still all around, but slacking off. Warden examined the darkness that held the row of hooches. There were no muzzle flashes. An illumination flare burst over Can Duoc. The flares didn't throw much more light than a full moon. He still couldn't see past the first line of hooches and brush. Lt. Stewart sent the order over the radio to use the hand-launched flares. Warden could just make out the movement of Sgt. Braden's squad pulling back to the dike the rest of the platoon were using for cover. The pop and crackle of small arms fire increased. The lull in the firefight was over. There was another battlefield sound—helicopters. Sgt. Warden could tell what kind of choppers were in the air by the sound—a pair of Cobra gunships. When he heard the sound of the Cobras, he pictured the way they hung forward in flight, like they were sniffing the terrain, seeking out prey. He pictured the two pods of rockets, the 7.62 mm Gatling gun protruding from the nose plus the 40 mm grenade launcher hanging underneath. The firepower of a pair of Cobras was awesome, magnificent to an infantryman.

The thump of their rotors was closer. Warden thought the CO must have called them when they first came under fire. He launched a hand flare. There was a crescendo of incoming small arms fire. Another 105 mm flare popped overhead just before the first one dwindled. The CO then gave the order to mark their positions with strobe lights. That meant the gunships were for them. They wouldn't be pinned down in the middle of a rice paddy much longer, which was good, since their left flank was exposed. There was a foot-high dike between them and the village, but only flat, dry paddy to the brush line and canal on their left. He thought of the Vietcong machine gunner. He was dead; or busy changing his position by floating his machine gun along the canal bank in a dugout. If he set up in the brush line just on second platoon's left rear they'd be fucked. Charlie could see them by flare light from the shadows of the brush and hooches.

Sgt. Warden didn't want to start that strobe. That would make him a target, but he had to or the gunship pilots wouldn't know where his squad was. The last flare burned out. The gunships circled, looking for the strobes that marked their positions. The lieutenant's strobe was flashing off to Warden's right. He couldn't see the command post's strobe. *Where the fuck was first and third platoon*? He laid flat, took off his steel pot, and set the strobe light in the bottom. He pressed the big rubber nipple to start it flashing. His steel pot/strobe arrangement directed the flash up, so it was hard for Charlie at ground level to tell exactly where it was. The CO was giving fire direction to the gunships. Sgt. Braden's strobe was going. They set them to flash every two seconds. The Cobras were off to his right rear lower and turning to line up on the village for their first run. They all knew what was coming next, except for George.

The rest of his squad was flattened out behind the dike to protect themselves from the rocket shrapnel. The rattle of AK rounds peaked. He yelled, "George, cease fire…get the fuck down. Now, George! Now!" The Cobras would start their runs in a few seconds. The pop of rifle fire stopped. He grabbed the strobe from his steel pot and tossed it to his right rear then rolled his steel pot back onto his head just as the lead Cobra opened up with rockets and the Gatling gun spewing four thousand rounds per minute. *Shit, they're close*. He felt concussions from the rockets detonating. A thought crept into his head. *What's it like, twenty yards away in those hooches*? The lead Cobra banked hard left. The second Cobra started its run. This time, as the second Cobra passed in front, he looked over the dike. He saw the gunship was hitting a line of brush just at the edge of the grass huts. The instant the second Cobra stopped firing, the rattle of AKs started again, and rounds were popping past.

Warden yelled, "Woody, give me the horn." He broke in on his lieutenant, Blue One, talking to the CO. "That's not where the VC are. We are still taking fire."

"Is that correct, Blue One?"

"This is Blue One, I…I don't know."

A pause, then the CO's voice. "Blue Two" that was Sgt. Warden, "you direct the gun ships."

The Cobras were making a wide turn to Warden's rear. He said. "This is Blue Two. Affirmative." He reached for his strobe and increased its flash rate to twice per second. "Firefly, this is Blue Two. I'm the center strobe flashing faster."

"I see you, Blue Two." The lead Cobra was turning back toward the village, its mate right behind.

"Firefly, this is Blue Two. Fire direction. Add ten meters. Same line. Over."

"This is Firefly, Roger."

The Cobras were turning to line up on Can Duoc village one more time. Sgt. Warden had directed the fire right down a row of huts. That meant civilians would die. The gunship pilot didn't use his call sign—there was no time. "Blue Two. Blue Two. ARE YOU SURE?"

Sgt. Warden recognized Firefly's voice. Just before he answered, he felt, more than heard, a quiet voice inside him.

Stop. Don't do this. It's wrong.

Sgt. Warden keyed the handset.

"I'm sure…Make the run."

Before he released the handset switch, the lead gunship opened fire. His head was still above the dike and he saw the line of hooches explode. The second gunship was lining up and would start his run in a few seconds. Warden should have gotten down, but he couldn't look away. The second gunship opened fire. Sticks and straw and chunks of earth erupted from the village. Can Duoc began to burn. The peasants didn't have a prayer against the dragons he unleashed. The firefight was over.

There was small arms fire still coming from the village. *What the fuck. Was that fire coming from first and third platoon on the other side of the village? It sure as hell wasn't coming from the burning hooches on this side.* He scanned the village, looking for muzzle flashes. A man jumped from a smoking hooch and ran toward him. Before the man could raise his arms over his head George began firing. The man waved his arms over his head once and slumped to the ground. Warden could tell the man was unarmed and now he was dead.

"I got one!" George yelled. The fucking new guy had turned to look at Sgt. Warden with his saucer-sized eyes.

Now he knew George had what it took to kill a man. And Sgt. Warden knew something about himself: he had what it took to massacre a village. He heard rifle fire popping and whizzing around him. Warden took the radio handset from Woody. *How could I have done this?*

He yelled into the mike "Cease fire! Cease fire! We're shooting at each other through the village. Cease fire!" He was no longer afraid to die. He deserved to die. The last flare burned out. Starlight washed the silent huts. Sgt. Warden watched, detached at first, then immersed in what he had done. The men of Alpha Company lay behind the dikes in the rice paddies and waited for the sun.

At dawn, Alpha Company moved in to search the village. Without asking his lieutenant, Sgt. Warden took his squad into the village first. He walked point. He felt it was only right, since he was responsible for what they were about to see. The first thing he saw when he entered the village was a mamasan on her knees sobbing. Before he could walk past her, she raised up, her eyes locked his. "*Tai sow! Tai sow*!" (Why! Why!)

Sgt. Warden knew the answer. He had lost his compassion. He had dehumanized the villagers. He had put the need to survive before anything else. Tom Warden knew the instant he keyed the mike and spoke the words "I'm sure. . . Make the run," He had made a clear choice to abandon himself to the madness and survive at all costs. Sgt. Warden turned away and walked farther into the village with a question of his own. *Survival as what*?

Now there was a different fear. A fear of living with what he had done. He listened for that quiet voice he'd heard last night. It was not there. In its place was a sobbing for something sacred that had died. The boy from Indiana who just wanted to know what made the corn grow was gone. The child was dead. The man was dead. He had not survived. Tom Warden felt the pride and shame of being a good soldier. Underneath that feeling there was another. He could not go home…not ever.

Laura's Garden

Saturday, September 28th, 1984: Acushnet, Massachusetts

Sarah went around the side of the cottage to see if Laura was in the garden. Godiva, Laura's Collie, came around the corner of the fenced garden and greeted Sarah. She went through the gate and gave Godiva a good scratch behind the ear. Godiva looked into the garden and barked twice.

Laura looked up from her work. "I'm busy, girl."

Sarah came up behind her, "How you doing, Laura?"

"Oh, Sarah. Hi."

"Thought you'd be in the garden."

"Yes, she needs a lot of attention this time of year."

"Don't we all."

Laura tilted her head and smiled. "Some more than others. Come on in, honey. You can help me with the weeding." Sarah stepped onto the stone path that wound through the garden. Grass grew up through the stones, along with a few yellow dandelions. Laura stood and gave Sarah a hug. She adjusted her black and yellow kneepads before kneeling back down to work.

"You have to be careful not to pull up any useful herbs. They look like weeds, but they are so special. I suppose the weeds are special, too, but we just don't know what they have to offer. Like this one. Crabgrass. What use could it be? It does hold the soil together, though." Sarah knelt, accepted a gardening trowel from Laura, and engaged the patch of crabgrass. "Get down to the roots, dear, or it will just come back and try to take over your life."

Sarah drove the tool deep and stopped. "You mean take over the *garden*?"

"Well, you know what I always say, 'Life is like a garden. It needs tending'." Laura sat back a little and looked out over the garden. "I knew a man who let his garden get *so* out of hand—just *full* of thistles. He plowed the whole thing up and started over. It worked, I guess. No more weeds, but there was a lot of bare ground for awhile."

Laura returned to digging crabgrass with just a little more determination. "So much work, seeding all that bare ground. He didn't get it all done the first spring and the thistles came back up." Laura stood up and turned to Sarah. "He plowed up too much at once. Men are like that." She pointed at the center of her chest. "When *I* dig up a patch, I always put in what I want growing there."

She looked past the back garden fence, which bordered a stream that fed Noquochoke Lake. "There's plenty of wild ground outside the garden." Sarah was pulling the loose clumps of crabgrass from the earth. Laura set a basket down for her. "Put the old grass in here. I use it in the mulch pile. At least it's good for that." Sarah placed the clumps of drying crabgrass into the basket, then stroked the ground and picked out bits of roots.

When the basket was full, Laura carried it to the mulch pile, stepping over a shrub as she went, then walked back toward the house past Sarah, up the steps, and into the back room where she washed her hands in the deep porcelain sink. Sarah followed and washed her hands also. The big brown bar of lye soap felt awkward in her hands. When she finished, she held her hands out and looked for a towel.

Laura took one of Sarah's hands and toweled it off, roughly at first, and then more slowly. When she had carefully dried each finger, Laura placed Sarah's arm to her side, then did the same for Sarah's other hand. Sarah's lips were sealed against a sob, her eyes closed against tears. Laura shifted back a half step and watched Sarah's body.

Sarah raised her hands. Before her hands hid her face, a cry broke from her. More than a sobbing—an anguish. Laura held Sarah's wrists as she sank to her knees drawing in air. She knelt in front of Sarah and pulled her close. Sarah sobbed herself to exhaustion and settled back on her legs. Laura released her, then retrieved the hand towel from the lip of the sink. Sarah took the towel and wiped her face. Laura raised herself with a hand on the counter and opened the faucet to run some cold water. Sarah got up and went to the sink, still breathing deep. She washed her face, picked a fresh towel off the shelf over the sink, and dried herself.

Laura said, "So, is there something bothering you, Sarah?"

"Oh, maybe." Sarah said, almost smiling.

"Come sit." Laura stepped up and through the doorway leading into the kitchen. She pulled out a chair for Sarah and sat at the corner of the kitchen table.

Sarah sat down and ran her fingers over the red, blue and yellow flowers painted on the white tabletop.

"Tom and you OK?"

"Yes…we're OK. I thought I wanted us to stay that way. I wanted us to be OK forever."

"Hmm." Laura began to unbraid her hair.

"Now Tom wants to get married…I think. He said he would if that's what I wanted." She placed her right hand flat on the tabletop as if she were taking an oath. "Actually, he said he wanted to marry me, but didn't really ask me to marry him."

"What did you say?"

"Nothing. I didn't say anything. When he was leading up to the marriage thing, he said I would be a wonderful mother."

"That was a nice thing to say. Do you think he's right?"

"No. I told him so. I told him I didn't have any interest in abandoning my daughter. He picked up on that. I didn't say abandon my *child*. I said abandon my *daughter*."

"Well, not so surprising, is it?"

"You mean since my mother abandoned me, I believe I'd do the same to my daughter?"

"That's pretty much how we learn when we're children and think the world revolves around us."

"What are you saying? That it was selfish of me to expect my mother to stay around, to take care of me?"

Laura reached for a big cookie jar on the counter behind her. She opened it and held it out to Sarah. Sarah took one. Laura held the cookie jar in her lap.

"Your mother didn't abandon just you when she took her own life. It wasn't just about you."

"Maybe, maybe…but the part that *was* about me still hurt. What could you know about that anyway? You weren't there. I don't understand. I don't want to talk about it."

"I'm sorry. I can see that you've got some roots there. I didn't mean…"

"I *know* I'm still angry about my mother, but so what. I don't have to go there. You know? I can say it's just not worth going for the roots. Isn't that a way to do it?"

Laura took a bite of cookie and spoke around it. "You can, I suppose." She reduced the bite of cookie and swallowed. "Everybody talks about getting to the root of the problem though."

"Well I *know* I can just cut the tops. I *have* been. Why can't Tom just never mind about me being a mother? I don't ask him to play the piano or be a lawyer. Why does he ask me to be something that is agonizingly hard for me?"

Laura drew in a purposeful breath, left the table and went into the front room. She sat near the front window. Sarah followed and stopped just inside the archway.

Laura continued looking out the window. "You know you shouldn't do anything concerning your being a mother *for* Tom, or *because* of Tom, or anybody but yourself. Tell me something, are you saying you wouldn't be a good mother for unselfish or selfish reasons?"

Sarah ran her fingertips along the curved surface of the grandmother's clock. "How about if I'm pregnant? Should I consider the unborn?"

Laura turned to look at Sarah. "Have you tested yourself?"

"Yes."

"And?"

"I'm pregnant. Almost two months."

"You haven't told him?"

"No. I don't think I'm going to."

"Well Sarah, did he say he would be willing, or wanted to raise a child with you."

"Wanting and willing aren't enough. He has to be capable."

"Yes…and you don't think Tom is capable of being a father?"

"I think Tom would be a better mother than a father."

Laura started to laugh, then said, "I'm sorry. This is a very serious thing, but that is just too funny not to laugh. It's such a comical picture. Anyway, is there a chance he could handle the responsibility?"

Sarah turned, walked across the room and stood near Laura then began pacing in front of the windows. "There is always the chance, but why take the chance? There are enough children with bad parents. Why make more?"

"A very grim view of yourself and Tom."

"Well, hell. Do you know all the different jobs he's had in the last ten years?" Laura opened her palms. Sarah continued. "Twelve. He can't hold a job. Not *won't*, but *can't*. I've seen him working and just stop and stare into space. He's good when he's up, but a burden when he's down." She moved the edge of the blue lace curtain aside and peered into the yard. "I've never seen him angry, but I know he gets angry. He simmers or goes off by himself to do I don't know what. Sometimes, I think, to get drunk." She turned away from the window and raised her arms. "Sometimes he's just great. Wonderful. Then without any warning he goes blank." She dropped her arms to her sides.

"Sarah, do you think you could raise a child by yourself?"

"Maybe." She folded her arms. "I don't want to though. I'm selfish…like my mother."

"Yes, Sarah, there is always that. I'm going to ask you to do something. Something just for you. Because I don't think you've been completely honest." Laura traced a finger over the window sill. "Isn't it possible that you are using your alleged inability to be a good mother as an excuse for an abortion? Instead, why not just say, 'I like my freedom. I don't want to be tied down raising a child'. There's nothing wrong with that, Sarah. You would probably feel good."

"It would feel like a big argument with my sister-in-law and of course a major sin." She folded her hands in prayer in front of her and rolled her eyes at the ceiling. "A sin punishable by eternal damnation."

Laura raised a finger to the ceiling and stood. "Oh boy, that eternal damnation thing is always coming up. Temporary damnation or eternal, it kind of puts a damper on free will." Laura walked over to the piano, put her left hand on it for a moment, then sat and positioned herself to play. She sent a train of rising notes into the room. "Free will is a tricky thing, Sarah. We think we want it, but it is such a heavy responsibility really. I don't think we are given free will. I think it is forced upon us. It is part of the bargain, don't you think?"

"Bargain, what bargain?"

"The one we eventually have to make with life if we're going to have any peace of mind or satisfaction from life."

Sarah looked down at her stomach, put her left hand there, and looked at Laura. "We don't have much free will before we are born, do we?" She sat on the piano bench next to Laura. She protected her midsection with her arms and waited with a frown.

"I'll bet you are thinking about taking care of this all by yourself, but really, you should talk to Tom." She played a few high notes as she spoke. "A very delicate business."

"I don't know if I can do that. I'm afraid to talk to Tom about this, but I know I have to. It's only right…and I will."

Laura experimented with a few more notes on the piano then began to play. Sarah put her hands on her knees and raised herself up from the piano bench, turning toward Sarah. "I have to get back to work." Laura nodded and played the piano. Sarah left through the front door and went to the Blue Oyster.

Life Goes On

Saturday, September 28th, 1984: Fairhaven, Massachusetts

When Sarah arrived at the Blue Oyster, she noticed Tom's truck was there. She went around back and in through the stock room. When she got to the kitchen, she saw his legs sticking out from behind the Viking stove, which was pulled away from the wall.

"You OK?"

"Sort of. A little awkward getting behind here." Tom grunted. "There, we have gas to the stove." He pushed himself out from behind the stove. "Think we can shove this back together?"

"Let's give it a bid." They shoved on one corner and it moved a little.

"The other side," Tom said.

The stove moved again and they continued to walk it back against the wall. "OK let's try it." Tom opened a burner valve to bleed the air. *Tick tick,* the igniter sparked. Tom stepped back from the stove. The burner lit. "How was gardening?" Tom asked as he tried all the burners.

"OK. We talked, mostly."

"Oh?"

Sarah boosted herself up onto the stainless steel worktable next to the stove. "Tom?"

"Yes, Sarah?"

She brushed some dirt from the garden off her knees and looked over at Tom. "Sometimes you seem really…peaceful. Other times…wired up, strung out."

Tom picked a wrench up off the floor and looked across the stove at Sarah. "I don't like being that way. Seems like I can't do anything about it, though, if that's what you're asking."

"Well…yes. I'm not telling you that you *have* to change. I guess I'm just wondering if you ever will." Sarah scooted off the counter. "You're not just going to wake up some morning and have everything be OK. You have to do something." She thought she saw Tom's eyes narrow. She shifted her weight forward and peered up at him. "What do you think, Tom?"

His eyes searched the floor and found the toolbox just behind Sarah. Stepping around her, he knelt down and opened it. Sarah didn't move. He placed the wrench in the toolbox, closed the lid, and latched it. "I never really thought about it. I guess I really do think everything will be different in the morning. I…I'm just so relieved when I get through another day, and so I just keep doing it. Then years go by. I feel like I haven't got much time left, and then another day happens." Tom half rose, then sat on the toolbox, facing away from Sarah.

Sarah turned just enough to see him, wanted to touch him, to straighten his rounded shoulders, but didn't .

She spoke to the floor in front of her. "Did Mara, the counselor in Boston, help?"

"Some, I guess. It was better than the other times."

"What other times?"

Tom stood up. "It was about five years ago, before I came here, I went to a psychiatrist."

"What? She jerked around and looked down at him. "Why didn't you tell me that?"

He turned his head, and looked up at her. "I didn't want you to know I had…mental problems."

"Oh, like I was going to miss that?"

Tom smiled and shrugged his shoulders. "I went to a Dr. Stump, at the VA Hospital in Indianapolis."

"What? Dr. *Stump*? At the VA hospital?"

"I swear to God, Sarah, that was his name."

"He should have changed it to something else."

"I think he changed it to Stump to desensitize the amputees."

"That's not funny, Tom."

"Dr. Stump told me the only way to get back into life was to relax and forget about the war. He gave me a prescription for an anti-anxiety drug."

"Did it help?"

"Sort of. But when I was taking it, I didn't feel like myself, so I stopped taking it.

"Wasn't that the idea? To feel different than the way you were feeling?"

"There's more to it than that. When I was taking it, I had less anxiety in general, but I didn't worry about dying as much either. So, the idea of suicide didn't bother me as much, and with that door opened, I got scared again. Anyway, the anti-anxiety drugs didn't really take away the fear. Hard to explain."

He put his hands in his pockets and took a few steps, facing away from Sarah. "I remember I would drive really fast on the back roads. I was still scared, but I *liked* the feeling. When I talked about the anger, that black rage I would get, he gave me Thorazine. I took one. I remember when it wore off I had never been so depressed in my life! I wanted to die, but didn't have the energy to kill myself. So I don't know what to do, Sarah." Tom went over to the stove and shut off all the burners.

Sarah took a moment to absorb what he had just said. She knew he was in Vietnam, but had never thought of him as a war veteran. When he turned away from the stove and stepped toward her she met his eyes.

"Did you ever kill anyone?"

Tom stopped dead in his tracks, blinked once, and just stood there, looking at her.

She looked away. "I'm sorry. I shouldn't have asked that." She looked at him again and inched closer. "Sorry…I know it was tough for you. I never really thought about it before. I suppose being in combat is the closest thing to rape a man can experience."

They looked at each other, both wondering why the stranger in front of them felt so familiar.

Sarah spoke first. "You're lucky to be alive with all your arms and legs."

Tom sighed, started nodding his head, and looked through her. "You don't know how lucky." She watched his face go slack and the light leave his eyes. "Me and my point man were real lucky one day. Not totally lucky. I got a concussion."

Sarah wasn't sure what to do, but she didn't want him to stop talking. She asked, "You were in the hospital then?"

"No…no. I was still walking around. I was OK. Standing up and not bleeding from the ears so carry on."

Sarah scooted back onto the stainless steel counter, gripped the edge with her hands and leaned forward. Tom kept looking at the spot where Sarah had been standing.

"The guy following me stepped on a land mine and got his legs blown off. Died three days later. Guy behind him took shrapnel in the head. Died on the medevac chopper. Guy behind him got knocked unconscious; lived, though. He used to walk point. Probably felt safe walking fifth that day, but I guess he wasn't."

Tom turned and scanned the room behind him. He took a half step backwards, inching toward Sarah. He turned, walked to the worktable and sat down next to her.

Sarah folded her arms across her stomach. "I know that feeling…of not being safe. Not being able to protect the ones I love. Maybe that's why I don't want to become attached."

More to fill the silence than anything else, Tom said, "I didn't think I was going to make it out of Nam. Then I started to believe I would die there. Believing I would die soon got to be a habit."

"That's a habit you can break. Isn't it?"

"I never thought of it that way, as breaking a habit."

"Laura told me that if I plan something far enough in the future I would get in the habit of picturing myself in the future."

"Laura said that?"

"Yes." Sarah nodded her head. "Laura said a lot of things…about the future."

Tom rolled his eyes at the ceiling. "There, you see. Even thinking about planning something has got me upset. I feel…I feel…"

"What?"

"Smothered. Like I'm covered in wet blankets. I just feel drug down. Feels like tunnel vision, like tunnel thinking…Yeah." Tom got up and started putting his tools back in the toolbox.

When he'd finished Sarah said, "I told Laura you didn't ask me to marry you, but you offered to marry me."

"What did she say to that?"

"I forget, exactly. But when you offered, it sounded like a life sentence for you."

Tom held his hammer in both hands, looking at it like he didn't know what it was. "It would be hard for me…for me to always be there for you…and a family. I don't feel like I could hold up. You know what I mean?"

"Yes…like when you need to go off by yourself."

"Yeah, like those times. Yesterday I felt like if I had the responsibility, I could just push through and then maybe, like you said, get in the habit of feeling good." Tom closed his toolbox and looked up. "Why all the questions? Are you trying to fix me?"

"No. I was just thinking about what you said about us having children."

"You don't think I would make a good father, do you?"

"I think you would make a wonderful father…when you're OK. When you're not OK you're not wonderful at all."

"Yeah, I know. I wouldn't be a good father, not a good husband either. Not a good anything. The worst thing is that I don't know how long the bad spells are going to last. I just ride them out. We don't have to worry about that now, do we?"

"Well Tom, maybe we do."

"Why?"

"I'm pregnant."

Tom stepped closer to Sarah, looked at her stomach and her eyes.

* * *

"Don't worry, I'm not going to have the baby." Tom just looked at her. "Look, Tom, no matter what you think you can do about being a father, I'm afraid the extra pressure and responsibility *would* put you over the edge. Besides, I don't want to be tied down. Especially if it means being a single mother. You don't even have a steady job. Finger and I don't give health insurance."

Tom put his hands in his pockets and looked around the room. Sarah walked around in front of him.

"I'm going to have an abortion. I have the seven hundred dollars."

She waited. Watched him as his face lost expression. *There it is, that God damn blank stare*. She hated it. She knew the conversation was over. She might as well be talking to the wall.

When he finally spoke the monotone of his voice felt cruel.

"When? I'll take you."

"No. I don't want you there. I want to be alone."

"...OK."

"I go the day after tomorrow. In the morning."

"Is it safe for you to drive?"

"I'll be fine." Sarah picked up her satchel; put the strap over her shoulder. "Laura can come get me if I need someone." She strode to the back door and left.

* * *

Tom wanted to stop her. Felt he should stop her. Felt he was supposed to stop her, but felt powerless. *My main source of income is illegal. I live in her house. The shrinks say I'm crazy and maybe should commit myself to an asylum for evaluation. That's all the commitment I'm capable of.*

He went to his toolbox, opened it and wondered what it was he wanted from his toolbox. He took out the top tray, looked, dropped the tray and looked around the room. He went out the back door and walked to his pickup. Two steps away, he gathered some momentum, rose up, and slammed his palm into the driver's side window, holding back just enough so the window, or his hand, wouldn't break. He had learned to use the heel of his palm instead of his fist to avoid permanent injury. *Ha! I can still control the rage.*

Tom Warden stepped away from the truck, put his head down and began walking. He didn't stop till he got to the beach at Fort Phoenix. He looked out across the Atlantic Ocean and thought about a toy sailboat he made so many years ago. He remembered how he would send it sailing across the pond near the farm, then run to the other side and wait for it to come ashore.

The Old Man's Hooch

August 1969: Republic of South Vietnam

Alpha Company was spread thin. They were sweeping through an area of rice paddies bordering the rubber plantations near Xuan Loc. Second platoon had the left flank. Sgt. Warden's squad was on the left flank of second platoon. The trees and brush on the dikes made visual contact between the platoons impossible. Sgt. Warden could not even see the rest of his platoon at this point. He knew being separated from the firepower of the rest of the company was not a good thing. Letting this place remind him of a quiet afternoon back on the farm was not a good idea either, but he let the memory creep in. He began to feel more like a farm boy than a soldier. It only heightened his feeling of separation from home.

His squad was split into two fire-teams. Warden had moved to the far left of his squad and was watching a hooch even farther to their left. It was built on a platform about three feet above the rice paddy. There was a man sitting on the raised platform. He was watching Warden. Warden stopped and faced him. The man, dressed in black pajamas, waved his hand, palm down, and indicated the space opposite him on the platform.

Warden turned to Woody, his RTO, and said, "I'll be right back."

His M-16 was slung at hip level, his hand on the pistol grip and finger on the trigger. He flicked the selector from full auto to safe, then un-slung his weapon and cradled it with his left arm. He felt his fear rise as he approached the hooch. The old man just looked at the platform floor in front of him. Warden could see the opening of the hooch, but everything inside was lost in shadow. He stopped at the edge of the waist-high platform next to the spot the old Vietnamese man had indicated and saw a teapot and cups laid out on a cloth in front of him. He looked back at the dark opening and held his M-16 out across the deck, muzzle pointing at the dark doorway, hand on pistol grip, thumb on safety, finger on trigger. Every instinct told him to call his squad over and search the hut. Sgt. Warden took his finger off the trigger and laid his weapon down. He felt like he had been dismembered.

A wave of panic washed over him. If he got up on the platform and sat facing the old man, his back would be to his M-16 lying on the platform. He put both hands on the deck, boosted himself up and sat cross-legged facing the old farmer. He left his weapon lying behind him. The farmer looked at the soldier, smiled, and filled his cup with tea. He paused the teapot over the empty space between them, poured his own cup full and sat the pot on the cloth next to his knee.

They drank tea. The old man's gaze took in the hooch, the fields, the nearby trees. Sgt. Warden began to mirror his gaze, seeing the things he saw. His farm, his home, the birds that kept him company…

The old man never looked at him again.

Warden's squad was still moving. Woody yelled, "Hey, Sarge, come on!" Tom sighed, nodded to his host and slid off the deck. He reached back for his weapon and slung it low by his hip, hand on pistol grip, thumb on safety, finger on trigger. He flipped the fire selector to full auto and walked back toward his men.

As he got near, Woody said, "Let's go, Sarge, we're settin' up an LZ" and pushed ahead. The company was forming two columns on opposite sides of the next rice paddy. Zimmerman, the point man, was way out front humping toward the left flank of the LZ.

Warden knew he'd better *di di mau* if he was going to catch up. Woody caught up to the rest of the squad up on the dike leading to the LZ. Warden heard the choppers coming. He was ten feet from the dike when the familiar crack of a passing AK round snapped in his right ear and took a chunk out of the dike in front of him. A single reality filled his psyche. *Sniper*!

"What the fuck?" he said on his way to the ground. *That was a lousy shot for a sniper*. He stood up and looked back at the old farmer's hooch, about a hundred yards away. The old man was nowhere in sight, but Warden spoke to him anyway.

"My grandma could have made that shot."

He felt a bull's-eye on his chest. He stood there, understanding his life was not his. It felt like he was being swallowed by the universe.

Woody's voice broke the spell, "Come on Sarge! Get the fuck out of there!"

His squad was moving fast toward the LZ. Tom smiled, saluted the hooch, and walked off toward the LZ. He was in no hurry to get back to the war. He knew the soldier and the farmer had made a peace treaty, not so much with each other, but within.

Leaving the Garden

Monday, September 30th, 1984: Acushnet, Massachusetts

Sarah left the abortion clinic and drove to Laura's. She noticed Laura's car was not in the driveway, so she parked on the street. She slung her leather satchel over her left shoulder, exited the car, walked past the front porch and into the garden without stopping. She went over to the stone bench to sit then thought better of it and sat in the swing near the back of the garden. She placed her satchel on the swing next to her, opened it, slid out a notebook and began to write. There was no breeze. Sarah was glad for the vined trellis that shaded her.

When Laura came home, the sun was setting so she went immediately to the garden, grabbed her basket and began to gather kale and some cherry tomatoes. When she went back to check on the grapevines she discovered Sarah asleep in the swing. Laura sat on the stone pavers in front of the swing and began to hum. Sarah opened her eyes. She yawned sat up.

"Hope you don't mind me coming into your garden like this."

"That's perfectly fine, Sarah. What brings you here today?"

"I didn't know where else to go."

Laura got up, moved the satchel aside and sat next to Sarah. Their shoulders were touching.

Sarah looked at her hands folded in her lap. "I had the abortion this morning." The two women allowed the silence. They waited for the garden to absorb what had just been said. Sarah drew a breath.

Laura asked, "Can you talk about it?"

"They were all very nice, very professional. I thought I was ready." Sarah ran her fingers into her hair and held her head. "They put a tube in me and started to suck the fetus. I felt like everything inside me was being sucked out. Like there would be nothing left of me when they were done." She picked up her notebook and held it in her lap.

"What's that?"

"Something I wrote before you got here." Sarah tore a page from the notepad and looked at it.

"Can you share?"

Sarah held out the slip of paper. Laura took it and read silently.

Once a faint and fragile light you gave.
Like the Moonbeam, for a moment you were mine.
Then, unwanted, your soul wandered on,
Perhaps to another time, another place.
And now, forever, I will never know your face.

"This is beautiful, Sarah." She handed the paper back. "Will you read it to Tom?"

"I don't think so."

"Why not?"

Sarah looked at Laura, then through her. "Tom and I have suffered enough. No matter where we touch each other, we always find a scar." The slip of paper fell from Sarah's fingertips. As it fell, a whirlwind came through the garden and carried the poem up over the grapevines toward Tinkham Pond.

Laura stood, watched it go, then looked back at Sarah. Sarah tucked her notebook into the satchel, stood, then turned away from Laura. She left the garden, and drove home.

Sarah pressed the garage door remote as she rolled past Tom's truck in her driveway. She parked in the garage. *He's here. I'll have to talk to him about the abortion.* She slumped in the driver's seat and rested her forehead on the steering wheel.

* * *

Tom was in the spare bedroom he had set up as an office doing bookwork. He had been sleeping in the office/bedroom now for several weeks. When he heard the garage door open, he placed his pen on the desktop and rolled his office chair back. When Sarah didn't come in right away he got up and walked to the office door and waited. He heard the car door open and close. He waited. She came in, turned toward the back bedroom and stopped when she saw Tom.

"How you feeling?" he asked.

"Terrible. I didn't think it would be like this." She looked at the floor then back at Tom.

"You want to lie down?"

"Yes," she said, then went to her bedroom and sat on the edge of the bed.

Tom followed. “Did they give you any painkillers?” She nodded. “I’ll get you some water.” He got a glass of water from the kitchen and brought it back. Sarah had two pills in her hand.

She accepted the glass of water, took the pills and said, “They used a vacuum pump. It felt like all my insides were being sucked out. I didn’t think it would feel like this.”

“Do you want to talk?”

“No.”

Tom knelt down and untied the running shoes she always wore and took them off. Sarah got under the covers, folded her hands across her stomach, and closed her eyes.

“I’ll check on you later,” he said. He went to the kitchen and mixed up a pasta salad, which he divided into two bowls. He took one to the back bedroom for Sarah. She did not move or open her eyes. Her lips were slightly parted. Tom put the bowl of pasta salad on the nightstand, then went down the hall to his office. He sat on the edge of the bed, and tried to imagine how she felt. He could not.

Bravest Man In Nam

September 1969: Republic of South Vietnam

Combat units were being pulled out of South Vietnam. The troop withdrawals started back in June. Now the mission was *winning hearts and minds.* No more body counts. This was the Vietnamization of the war. The part where the United States told the Vietnamese, *You know what? This isn't working out. We've done all we can, so you need to suck it up and make us look good. Of course, we'll wait a decent interval before we leave completely.*

Sgt. Warden knew the United States, his country, had given up on Nam. Global politics was not on his mind, but he felt his country had deserted him as well as the Vietnamese. Somehow, he wanted an apology. He wanted someone to admit they made a huge mistake and now wanted him and men like him to stay on and clean up the mess. He knew there would be no apology. He also knew a change in strategy did not automatically mean a change in tactics. He knew the habits of war had become ingrained in him and in his men and, after all, the Vietcong and NVA were still trying to kill them.

Alpha Company had saddled up and filed out of the gate of the firebase at Binh Canh that morning about 9 am. From there they walked the half-mile on a dirt road into the village of Binh Cahn. It was a pacification mission. The village was not hostile. In the past nine months the only violence in the village had been a command-detonated land mine under a one-lane bridge. The driver of the truck on the bridge at the time survived. So the orders were to go through the village and politely roust everyone out of their huts and send them to the Alpha Company medics near the center of the village where they would receive a checkup and a half-pound bag of rice.

No one in Alpha Company spoke Vietnamese except the Chu-Hoi. The reason for that was, up until then, the mission at the small unit level was to get a body count. The soldiers of Alpha Company were used to killing Vietnamese, not talking to them. So Sgt. Warden passed on a phrase his men were to utter when they stuck their heads in a hooch, "Go see *bác sĩ.*" Half English and half Vietnamese. *Bác sĩ* was Vietnamese for doctor. The confusing part was that the CO was near the south end of the village with the company medics, totally unaware of the South Korean medical post at the north end of the village. Sgt. Warden didn't know what their mission was, but he had seen the Korean officer and a few ROK soldiers at that end of the village when his squad rode through in trucks. The end result was that all the Vietnamese went to the north end of the village and surrounded the South Korean doctor.

Somehow, Sgt. Warden, as usual, had gotten his squad out on the left flank as far from his platoon leader and the CO as possible. After Warden said, "Good morning" to a few Vietnamese families and sent them to *go see bác sĩ*, Sgt. Warden let his men mill around and basically go on break. He went from hut to hut, speaking to the occupants. "*Chào anh, no sweat,*" which meant,

Good morning, I'm not going to ransack your home or shoot you. This did not put any of the families at ease. There were, after all, six men outside their house wearing flak jackets, steel helmets, and carrying assault rifles and a machine guns.

About halfway through the village, Sgt. Warden decided to go back to the command post, get some of the half pound bags of rice, and hand-deliver them. He hadn't gone far when he came upon Lieutenant Welch from first platoon. Lt. Welch was yelling at Buzz, a rifleman.

"Get in there, soldier, and search that hut."

Buzz backed away from the lieutenant. "No! This is stupid. We have no right to go into these people's homes with guns and…"

"Get in there and search the hooch. That's an order."

"No fucking way," Buzz said and threw down his M-16 so hard it bounced and hit the lieutenant in the leg. Lt. Welch's eyes bulged and his mouth dropped open. Sgt. Warden stopped in his tracks. Everyone, soldiers and villagers alike, froze and watched Buzz and the lieutenant.

"Pick up that fucking weapon! That's an order!"

"No way. I quit. I surrender. I'm not going to carry a gun anymore."

"I'll court-martial you! I'll charge you with desertion! Pick…up…your…weapon."

Buzz folded his arms across his chest. "No. It's not my weapon and I'm not deserting. I'm still here. I'm just not going to carry a gun anymore. I have no intention of shooting anyone so, I…am…*not*…going to pick up a gun. Ever again…sir."

Welch turned to the soldier next to him, a short-timer. "Pick up Lassiter's weapon."

Brock said, "I ain't carrying Buzz's shit."

"Pick it up. Brock!"

"You pick it up," Brock said and walked off.

It was GIs two, Lieutenant zero. Not good for discipline. Lt. Welch didn't want to give another order that wouldn't be followed so he snatched up the M-16 and slung it over his left shoulder, then went into the hooch. Sgt. Warden walked over to Buzz and said, "I didn't know you could just quit like that."

"Me neither."

"What do you think they'll do to you, Buzz?"

"I don't really care what they do. I only know I'm not going to carry a weapon."

"You're a brave man, Buzz," Sgt. Warden said and walked off. He felt the M-16 slung under his right shoulder. It was not so much a part of him now, but it was still attached. Tom Warden wanted the clarity of an infantry sergeant. He didn't want this independent thinking. He knew a lack of discipline could cost lives and yet he knew it was the independent spirit of the American soldier that made them the most effective, honorable fighting men the world had ever seen. When backed by the will of America, there was no terror they would not face, no act of compassion or courage they were not capable of, no sacrifice they would not make without hesitation.

Now he knew they were alone. Knew they had been deserted. He knew the final act of selfless courage demanded from them would be to bear the shame of their nation.

Sgt. Warden walked back to his men with his bags of rice. He felt responsible for their lives, but could only increase their odds of survival. To do that he had to be an infantry sergeant, not Tom, not the boy from Indiana who only wanted to know what made the corn grow. He realized he was lost in thought while walking, instead of scanning for danger. A lapse of focus he could not afford. He looked up and forced himself into the reality of a combat zone. Without breaking stride, he uttered the soldier's prayer, "Fuck it. It don't mean nuthin'."

The CO ended up sending Buzz and Lt. Welch back to the main firebase at Long Binh. There was no disciplinary action. The CO did not want it to go on record that there were any discipline problems in his company. Captain Henderson made Lt. Welch the executive officer in the rear and assigned Buzz as the lieutenant's Jeep driver. The Captain made it clear that if there were any more problems, they would both be court-martialed.

Plans for No Future

Tuesday, November 26th, 1984: Boston, Massachusetts

On the drive up to Boston for his fourth appointment with his counselor, Tom realized it would be the last one. By the time he sat down in Mara's waiting room, all he wanted to do was get up and leave. He was poised on the edge of his chair when Mara opened her office door and stepped into the waiting room.

Tom stood. "Good morning."

"How are you, Tom?"

He looked at the door, then back at Mara. "OK."

* * *

Looking at Tom, Mara was reminded of a stray dog caught in a fenced yard. She said, "I'll make some hot chocolate. Why don't you go in and sit by the window?" She left the door open and went to the table against the wall where there was coffee and hot water for tea. She opened packages of hot chocolate, put them in mugs, and poured in hot water. With a mug in each hand, She turned around and saw Tom had not moved. She motioned toward the office door with a mug. "Shall we?"

* * *

"Oh. Sure," he said. He accepted a mug of hot chocolate as he went through the door into her office. She followed and closed the door. Tom slumped into the high-backed chair he favored near the window. He liked that spot. He could see the sidewalk across the street from the second story-window. He cradled his mug of hot chocolate and examined the sunlight and shadow. To Tom, the fall afternoon seemed like it was part of another life, like the world was getting colder and colder and it would just keep getting colder until nothing moved.

He raised his mug. Took a sip of hot chocolate and swallowed. His eyes filled with tears. Mara took the cup from him and set it on the small table next to him. He began to sob. Mara went to her desk and sat with her hands folded in her lap.

Finally, Tom released a shuddering sigh. "I don't know what it is."

Mara leaned forward a bit. "Can you describe it a little?"

"Well, yes. It's a feeling that... I don't know what it is."

"Where does it come from?"

"My guts."

"Does it have a name?"

"Regret."

"Ah yes, regret. Tell me something about it. Anything."

Tom used a tissue, looked at the window pane, and said, "I feel lost. Like a made-up word, like I don't make any difference. Maybe that's it. I didn't *want* to make a difference anymore, and I got my wish. I don't want to die, but I don't want to be responsible for anything, especially another life. Not my life or anyone else's. I'm just waiting. Waiting for something, for anything to happen. I don't know what to do. Then when something does happen, it doesn't make any difference. It's just false hope. Maybe I should go somewhere without distractions. Maybe go back to the place it all went wrong."

Mara shifted in her chair. Tom turned more toward her and spoke to the floor between them. "Maybe there is no such time or place. Maybe I'll have to go back through all of it piece by piece. God, I don't want to do that." He drank hot chocolate, looked at Mara and continued. "Why wasn't I paying attention while it was happening? How did I end up so far from home? Questions. No answers, only questions."

He examined his mug and drank more hot chocolate from it. Mara allowed the silence. Tom continued.

"Something is keeping me alive. It pushes. Keeps me awake. I try to make it stop, but it won't. It pulls me from dreams. Shows me my whole life at once. Sometimes only shows me freeze frames. It never, *ever* shows me what comes next."

He set his mug on the table next to the chair and looked back out the window. He seemed to be interested in something on the sidewalk. His attention came slowly back into the room, to pictures on the wall, a crack in the ceiling, a stain on the carpet. Mara shifted ever so slightly in her chair.

Tom looked at her and said, "I can't hold out against the memories much longer. I might as well let it all play back; and this time pay attention. Even if it has to play back a hundred times before I figure it out. It didn't all go wrong at once, I guess. The screw-ups are smeared out all over my life." He stood and took a step toward the window.

"I'm going to let the madness take me. It's the only hope I've got. Maybe the pain will die before I do. Maybe I'll write it all down so I don't forget it all again."

Mara straightened in her chair and waited.

"Well …that sounds a lot like a plan, or at least the beginnings of one. It makes sense except for the dying part." Mara barely smiled, Tom not at all.

"I'm leaving. Probably go to Arizona and visit my folks."

Mara swiveled toward her desk, and looked back through her notes. "I'm going to give you the name of a psychiatrist in Prescott, Arizona. I think you should make an appointment. There's no need for you to suffer."

Tom stepped over and took the slip of paper she offered and said, "Thanks." He carefully filled out a check to pay for the session and gave it to Mara.

She accepted the check. "Good luck Tom." Tom nodded and left the office.

He missed the turnoff that would take him past Taunton to Route 140 and on down to New Bedford. He went all the way to Wareham and took old Highway 6 back through Mattapoisett into Fairhaven. A block away from Sarah's, he could see the house was dark. He parked in the driveway, went in and locked the door behind him. He walked down the hall past his office. Sarah's bedroom door was open. He went in, sat on the bed, and began to untie his boots. Sarah rolled up on one elbow toward him, rubbed her eyes and said, "I didn't think you would come back tonight. I thought you had disappeared again."

Tom looked over his shoulder and said, "It started out that way." He pulled his boots off and rolled onto the bed, resting his shoulder against the headboard so he could look at her. "I don't want to just disappear anymore. I have to leave, but I don't want to just drop everything and go like I've always done."

"I understand, Tom. At least, I think I do. I don't want you to go, but I don't want you to stay either."

"Yeah, it's like that. We can't just keep hanging on, waiting for the end."

* * *

Sarah fluffed up her pillow and laid back down on her side, facing him without meeting his eyes. She wondered if what they felt in the beginning was compassion, not romantic love. She wondered if the intimate moments were only passionate escapes, providing a primal reassurance they were not alone in the world.

Tom scooted down, laid his head back on the pillow, closed his eyes and said, "I think I need to be alone for a while." Sarah thought it best not to comment.

Satori

October 1969: Republic of South Vietnam

The usual routine for Alpha Company was to send out squad-sized patrols at night to set up ambush positions along the canals and dikes that could possibly be used as infiltration routes to get material in close to Saigon and Tan Son Nut, the American airbase. The ambush positions served as listening posts to spot the flash of rockets launched by the VC into the airbases and rear echelon installations. Word came down early that day that Alpha Company would mount a company-sized airborne operation in the pineapple groves west of Saigon. This was a known infiltration route and weapons cache area. VC and some NVA had been spotted in the area. Alpha Company would recon with a search and destroy mission. They would take trucks to the LZ about a mile from their patrol base at Binh Canh. The flight of choppers would pick them up there, then put them down far enough from the suspected NVA position to have a cold LZ.

Alpha Company was in the pineapple groves by noon and moving out in three columns. Sgt. Warden's squad had point on the right flank. Warden could visualize the setup. He had reviewed the area map with Lt. Vail that morning. He could see the brush line along the big dike ahead that intersected a canal on his left. There was a dike bordering the canal, also. They would move up to the dike, then turn toward the canal with the dike on their right.

The bad news was, to him it looked like they were moving into the receiving end of a perfect "L" ambush. That's where the enemy came at you from the front and from the flank. To make matters worse, this was an old pineapple grove. There were large dikes, like the one on their right, about every hundred feet. They were three feet high and five feet wide, perfect for hiding bunkers and spider holes. In between these large dikes were smaller parallel dikes where the pineapples grew. Those dikes were about two feet high and six feet apart. That provided good cover from either side, but made a shooting gallery from the front, and they were the targets. Just to make things interesting, there was about six inches of standing water between the smaller dikes.

Sgt. Warden and his squad moved toward the dike bordering the canal. They were parallel to and about fifty feet from the larger dike on their right. Warden could see the brush line along the canal on the other side. When his point man got close to the dike to their front, Sgt. Warden was going to have him swing left, which would put his squad facing the dike in front and linked up with the rest of Alpha Company on the left. First and third squad would make up the right flank.

Anticipating that maneuver, Sgt. Warden moved up even with his point man and off to the left, effectively linking up with first and third platoon, forming an assault line. The CO had set up Alpha

Company in anticipation of being ambushed. If the VC were in bunkers along the big dikes and sprung an ambush now, Alpha Company was almost too close to the big dikes for gunship support. Sgt. Warden felt the purple haze of fear rise. The men of Alpha Company moved with a stalking crouch, like a pride of lions hunting. The first crack of AK-47 rounds sent them diving for cover. In the next heartbeat, they were returning fire. A Chi-Com machine gun sprayed them from a bunker located in the corner of the "L" where the big dikes met. *Nearly perfect, but they should have waited till we were about thirty feet closer.*

Lt. Vail was shouting at the first and third squads to pull back from the big dike on the right flank. That would leave enough distance between them and the dike for a Cobra gunship to make a run without losing anyone to friendly fire. Sgt. Warden crawled back to Villalobos and shoved a box of M-60 linked ammo at him. Villalobos grabbed it and passed it over to Phil, who was putting twenty-round bursts into the VC bunker in the corner.

Sgt. Warden and all of third platoon were pinned down between the little dikes. They had cover from the right flank, but any VC on the big dike in front could shoot them down, no problem. Third platoon had reloaded and were starting a frontal assault on the bunker line. Warden's point man had gotten up, firing, to join the assault. Warden yelled at him, "Bart! Get back here! Get the Fuck back here. That's not our platoon!"

Bart kept going. Sgt. Warden finished arming the LAW he carried for just these occasions. The VC machine gunner had turned his attention to the third platoon assaulting and caught them in a crossfire. Sgt. Warden rose up on one knee, putting his upper body above the smaller dikes where he could see the right flank, and aimed the anti-tank weapon at the muzzle blast coming from the VC machine gun. He was worried he wouldn't get the shot off before he was hit, but he did. The machine gun in the corner was silent Still the AK-47 fire was so intense, third platoon's assault had stalled.

Every firefight has its ebb and flow. After the first minutes of terror, both sides usually settle down to take stock of things. There was one of those lulls and third platoon pulled back with their wounded. Sgt. Warden's point man was back and Warden sent him back to Villalobos. Woody was back there, too, leaving Warden lying in the water between the low dikes. He was checking the big dike in front to see if he could spot a bunker.

He rolled over one dike to his right and a round cracked over his head. It came from a spider hole in front of him. He edged to his right. A round smacked the dike on his left. The grass between the dikes was too high for Warden to see over in his prone position. It occurred to him that he would die in the next few seconds. He felt more relief than fear. He took one last look at the world of the living. He could hear a bird's song above the rattle of gunfire. He saw a grasshopper crawling up a blade of grass, and felt his own life was insignificant. Warden had never felt so much at peace. The world was in slow motion, almost frozen in time. Tom Warden was not afraid of dying. There was peace there.

He chose to live. Rising up on one knee, not caring whether or not he got his shot off before he was killed, he took careful aim at his comrade in arms and squeezed the trigger. The lid of the spider hole flopped closed. The realization that he had survived washed over him along with the sounds of battle.

A pair of Cobra gunships lined up to make a run on the big dike on the right flank. Sgt. Warden popped smoke to mark the outside corner of Alpha Company's position. The Cobras made their pass on the right flank. They unloaded with miniguns, 40 mm rockets and 40 mm grenades, then they swung around on the other dike, using only miniguns, to cover Alpha company's withdrawal out of the kill zone. A perimeter was set up about five hundred yards away and the CO called for artillery. He "walked" it up and down the brush line along the canal where they had been ambushed. Alpha Company settled in for the night.

Sgt. Warden watched the stars and wondered what he would do if he actually survived the next two months and went home. The hint of a plan for the future began to form. The fear of death crept back in with it. He woke up Jefferson, the next man on guard, then went back to lie on his poncho. In his psyche and in his soul, the rage of combat intertwined with his loving reverence for life and the strength a soldier finds on

Death Ground. He turned his face away from the stars and wrapped his arms around his rifle, the only truth he was sure of.

Give Me Back My Gun

Saturday, December 14th, 1984: Fairhaven, Massachusetts

Tom parked his pickup behind the Ferry Café where The Roach had a second-story apartment. Even though Detective Roche believed he was not guilty of the murder of Timmy Furtado, others might not agree. Timmy had been killed with a large caliber handgun, a .45 auto. A .45 auto like the one Tom gave up to The Roach, the one with his prints on it and on the ammo in the magazine. He knew how easy it was to swap barrels, ejectors, and firing pins between Model-1911 .45 auto pistols so that marks on the bullet and marks on the ejected casings would match his weapon. He had motive and opportunity. The Roach had the evidence that could link Tom to the murder of Timmy Furtado and Tom wanted it back before he left town.

Tom wasn't sure what would happen next, but he didn't want anyone to know he was there if something went wrong. The bar was closed and there were no streetlights. He removed the dome-lite and put it in the glove box. He could barely see, but managed to find the outside stairs leading up to The Roach's apartment. Tom tapped on the door.

"Lenny?" No answer. He knocked again.

"Yeah, who is it?"

"It's Tom."

"The door's unlocked."

Tom opened the door and looked into the dark room. A lamp came on across the room. The Roach was stretched out in a recliner next to it. “What’s on your mind, Tom?”

“I was wondering if I could get my piece back.”

“I don’t know, Tom. Bobby says Finger still doesn’t want any bagmen carrying guns.”

Tom closed the door and walked over to The Roach. “I quit.” He dropped the brown bag of money in The Roach’s lap. The Roach looked in the bag and set it on the end table next to him.

“I’m leaving town, Lenny.”

“Just when I was getting to like you, Tom. I thought maybe we could be friends someday.”

“I hardly know you, Lenny, but I don’t think we could ever be friends.”

“You know me, Tom. You even like me. You just don’t like to admit it. Anyway, I trust you and that’s important between friends.”

“Why do you trust me?”

“Because I know who you are and I can trust you to be that. Nothing more, nothing less.”

Tom sat on the edge of the sofa opposite The Roach and said, “Do the guys know you’re a philosopher?”

“Nah, I’m an enigma to them. They’re afraid of me. They wouldn’t like me if they knew me, so I give them The Roach. It’s simpler for them, safer for me.” Lenny crossed his legs. “But you’re not afraid of me, are you, Tom?”

“I should be, but no, I guess I’m not.”

"That's because you know me and trust me to be what I am. Nothing more, nothing less."

"What about my .45?"

"That's what I'm talking about." The Roach eased himself out of the recliner and stepped to the sofa. He lifted a cushion beside Tom, pulled out a Model 1911 .45 auto and handed it to Tom, butt first. Tom took it. The Roach reached back under the cushion and brought out another .45 caliber Model 1911. He handed that one to Tom grip first.

Tom took it with his other hand. "What the fuck, Lenny?"

The Roach sat back down in his easy chair. Tom set one pistol on the sofa next to him and held the other with the slide tilted toward the lamp.

The Roach chuckled. "The serial numbers are ground off. I broke into the kitchen one night after you left your gun with me, and took it and some booze. Made it look like a robbery. I was gone most the night shooting pool, so I could tell Bobby I didn't hear nothing because I wasn't there."

Tom sat back in the sofa and said, "I thought you trusted me, Lenny. Which gun is mine?"

"I trust you with a loaded gun, Tom, not with the truth."

"You maybe shouldn't."

"Maybe not, but I do." The Roach pointed to the two handguns. "Those can be our secret. I don't think you can explain them to anyone. So since you're leaving town I think they should leave with you."

Tom shook his head. He dropped the clip from the first pistol onto the cushion, then ejected the round from the chamber and pulled the trigger. He cleared the second pistol the same way. Tom looked up at The Roach, replaced the loose rounds into each clip and slapped the clips back into the grips. The Roach went to the other end of the sofa. He pulled a brown paper grocery bag and a small white cloth pouch from under the cushion.

"Here's somthin' to carry those in, and a bag of money. One thousand three hundred and twenty dollars."

Tom accepted the bag and pouch. The cloth pouch looked like the ones Hack used. He put the weapons and money in the grocery bag, walked toward the door, and said, "Goodbye, Lenny."

"See you later, Tom."

"Not if I see you first." Tom picked his way down the dark stairway. The bulb from the dome light was in the glove box so he entered the truck in darkness and pulled the door closed behind him. He started the truck and eased it to the street before turning on the headlights. After driving about five blocks, he stopped in a residential area and stashed the bag of pistols and cash behind the door panel he'd rigged for the money pickups. A few porch lights were on. He did an automatic scan of the street, took a deep breath and headed for Sarah's house.

* * *

Detective Roche put his finger under the words he had just read and repeated them out loud. "He will win who prepares himself, then waits to take the enemy unprepared." He put his copy of *The Art of War* by Sun Tzu on the bedside table as he swung his legs off the bed and stood in one continuous motion. He was still dressed. He retrieved his badge and gun lying beside the well read-book, and drew an even breath. He left his apartment and drove to the Ferry Café to confront his brother, Lenny The Roach. He parked near the back steps, grabbed his flashlight and went up. He paused for a heart beat, opened the door and said, "How many .45 automatics do you own, Lenny?"

Lenny laid the book he was reading in his lap and said, "Took you long enough to figure it out, Theo." Roche walked to the couch and sat down facing his brother. He reached around to the small of his back with his right hand, gripping the, butt of his .45. In one fluid motion, like an artist makes a brushstroke, he drew the weapon, aimed it at his brother and cocked it while his left hand brought a throw pillow off the couch and covered the muzzle.

"We should talk,"

"OK, Theo. Let's talk."

"Did you kill Timmy and those two thugs?"

"You know I did, but you can't prove it. The evidence is on its way out of town."

"How many others? How many people have you killed, Lenny?"

"Not as many as you. Not nearly as many."

"Maybe not, but..."

"But the people you killed were all justified. Is that it?"

"Yes! The killing I did was lawful. It was justified."

"Same for me, Theo. Same for me."

Roche threw the pillow at his brother. Lenny caught it and slipped it behind his head. Roche put the muzzle of his weapon into the couch, thumbed the safety on, and eased the hammer down. Then he holstered it and sat back on the couch.

"I don't know what to say, Lenny."

"I know what Warden would say."

"Yeah? What would Tom Warden say?"

"Fuck it. It don't mean nuthin'."

Detective Roche rose from the couch, walked to the door, and placed his hand on the doorknob. "This isn't over."

"I know, Theo. I know." He watched his brother leave. Leonard Roche, AKA The Roach, picked up his copy of Joseph Conrad's *Heart of Darkness* and continued reading. It was 2:00 am.

* * *

When Tom came into the kitchen, he heard a muffled voice from the TV and saw a bluish-gray light coming from the bedroom door. He walked to the bedroom. "How are you, Sarah?"

She didn't look up. Tom went over, sat on the bed, and put his feet up. Sarah got up, switched off the TV. Then laid back down beside Tom, and hugged a pillow.

Tom looked at her, then the pillow.

"I'm sorry, Sarah. I'm sorry I couldn't…"

"I'll be all right. I always am."

Tom pulled his feet up and put his hands on his knees. "I thought we could be more than all right. I thought we could stay together. I really did." Tom cleared his throat and pulled a tissue from the box at the bedside table.

"You're not going to cry, are you, Tom?"

"Probably. I miss the time when we were in love and didn't know anything about each other."

"Life's not that simple."

"I think it is, Sarah. Maybe that's why we can't be together." He wiped his eyes, leaned over and kissed Sarah on the forehead. He sat up with his feet on the floor.

"Are you running away?"

"No, not this time. No, I'm searching. Going on a great adventure. I have to go, Sarah."

"I know, Tom. I know."

Tom gathered his things from the house. His tools were already in the truck. All the things he carried were in three large trash bags, which he tied under a tarp in the bed of his pickup. When he turned to go back into the house, Sarah was standing in the doorway in her red terrycloth bathrobe. He walked up to her. She held out her arms. They held each other. They were teary-eyed but didn't cry.

Sarah loosened her embrace and looked into Tom's eyes. "You'll stay in touch, won't you?"

"Yes, I'll let you know where I am."

She kissed him and went back inside. Tom got in the truck and backed out of the driveway.

Dead Man Talking

November 1969: Republic of South Vietnam

Sgt. Warden had a piece of good luck. Three weeks ago he had been assigned to the brigade's main firebase to serve as Alpha Company's supply sergeant. He slept on the second floor of a wooden barracks. The shrapnel holes in the floor and tin roof from rocket attacks didn't bother him that much. He was not humping the bush any more, and had less than thirty days to go. Alpha Company had some good luck, too. They were also back at the brigade's base on a three-day stand down.

Sgt. Warden was in the supply room. Shark had just put a Montagnard crossbow in his personal storage. Warden padlocked the storage room and went outside. Shark was sitting on the low sandbag wall surrounding the supply room and company headquarters.

"You're getting pretty short, aren't you?" Warden said as he sat down next to Shark.

"Yeah, Sarge, only forty-seven days left."

"Woody said you walked point yesterday. Why you still walking point?"

Shark shrugged.

"You're too short to walk point. You only got a month left in country. Why you walking point again?"

Shark looked at his boots. "We moved into a new AO last week. It's the rubber plantations north east of here."

"You mean over by Xuan Loc?"

"Yep."

"Didn't an APC get hit with an RPG there a few days ago?"

"Uh huh… but we were all riding on top so nobody got blown away."

"That was you?"

Shark grinned. "Yeah, and that motherfucker was loud too."

"Jesus, Shark!"

"It ain't safe anywhere these days, so I figured I might as well go back to walking point and train the new guy."

Warden stood up. "You want a beer?"

"Sure, Sarge." Shark sat up and looked at Warden. "You keep beer in the supply room?"

"For after hours only and it's closing time." Warden went back inside, then came out with two beers. Shark held them while he padlocked the supply room door. He accepted a cold one back from Shark and popped the top. Shark opened his beer and took a swallow. Warden lit two Marlboros and handed one to Shark. Even though they were in the middle of a brigade-sized firebase sitting between two buildings, both men cupped their smokes to hide the glowing tips from snipers.

"Sarge?"

"Yeah?"

"If I get blown away, I want you to have my stuff."

"What?"

"I want you to have the Montagnard crossbow and the machete I got out of a bunker."

"Don't talk like that, Shark. You sound like you ain't going back home."

"There's just no safe place any more. Boo-coo VC around Xuan Loc. Charlie Company has been making contact every day for a week."

"So stop walking point *and* stop clearing bunkers."

Shark stood up and faced him. "Wouldn't make any difference, Sarge. I don't think I'm going home."

Warden knew what was on the other soldier's mind. He knew the pattern well: willfully risking the body's death because the soul it held was not worthy of life.

Sgt. Warden dropped his eyes to the beer resting on his knee and said, "Shark…I think…I think you should fight to survive and go home."

Shark shrugged, tossed his cigarette into the butt-can beside the door. "Take care of my stuff, Sarge."

Tom wanted to talk him out of what he had planned but knew Shark had become addicted to the unnatural act of killing a fellow human being. He took a moment, met Shark's eyes, and nodded. Shark turned and walked off toward the EM club. The next morning, Alpha Company loaded their gear and themselves on deuce-and-a-half trucks and headed for the rubber plantations.

Three days later, Buzz came into the supply room carrying web gear and a helmet from the field. Warden recognized the helmet by the artwork on the camouflage cover. It was Shark's. Buzz set the gear down beside the storage room door and stood, looking down at it.

"How bad?" Sgt. Warden asked.

"Shark got his face shot off clearing a bunker."

"You got his rifle in the Jeep?"

"Yeah."

"You want me to get it?"

"Nah, Sarge, I'll get it."

Warden unlocked the weapons rack. Buzz came back in with Shark's M-16 and shoved it into the rack.

"Easy now, Buzz." Buzz grabbed the weapon out of the rack and slammed it back. He grabbed it again and slammed it back into the rack hard enough to crack the fiberglass barrel guard. "Buzz, I believe you just damaged government property. You could get court-martialed for that."

Buzz turned on his heel and went out the door. Sgt. Warden took the damaged M-16 out of the rack and began cleaning it. He regretted not trying to talk Shark out of his suicide by Vietcong. He also understood that for some of them, there was just no way they could ever go home.

Salome

Sunday, December 15th, 1984: Danbury, Connecticut

The monotony of motion soothed Tom, gave him the feeling he was doing something significant. He could drive and let his mind wander. Wandering was what he wanted. Moving on was the most important thing. It didn't bother him that he wasn't moving toward a certain place. What was important was that he was moving away from where he was. He didn't realize yet that no matter where he ended up, he would still be with himself.

He didn't miss his family or friends. Those people seemed like someone else's family, make-believe friends. When he was rolling down the highway, he didn't even miss Sarah. At the last pit stop he made, she caught up with him, though. He wanted her to be there with him now and still leave the rest of the past behind. That never seemed to work. He had to leave all or none of the past behind. To deny any part of himself, he had to deny all of himself. To suppress any emotion, he had to suppress all emotions. Motion seemed to be the answer. The sounds coming from the pickup rolling over the pavement engulfed Tom in a cocoon of time and space separate from all other existence. That's the way Tom liked it. It was his only sanctuary, a place where the past or future could not touch him.

Yet it was not a perfect hiding place. There was something riding with him, a longing to be taken back into the fold, to be part of the grand cosmic experiment of life. Alongside this was the knowledge that he had killed without hesitation or remorse and had looked upon the dead and dying without compassion. He had accepted his own death as insignificant, like a leaf falling from a tree in autumn.

A part of Tom's mind registered an exit sign and the accompanying overpass ahead in the darkness. His foot increased the pressure on the accelerator and his thoughts ran for the shadows they came from. The outside world assembled itself into sharp reality. He eased the steering wheel to the left and aimed the pickup at the concrete pillars supporting the overpass. When the left front tire rumbled off the road, Tom savored the feeling of being neither alive nor dead. He allowed his arms to steer the pickup back toward the shoulder. The pickup rushed past the concrete pillars back onto the pavement. He eased off the accelerator and rolled down his window. Tom craved the infrequent clarity when the present world matched the constant fear he felt inside him. When several miles and the adrenaline were behind him, he scanned the gauges on the dash and noticed he was low on fuel. He took the next exit that had a beckoning gas station.

A young woman with raven hair sat on the curb at the entrance to the station. She watched Tom get out and walk inside. He came out and started filling his tank while looking up at the stars. The young woman picked up her duffel bag, walked over and sat her bag down beside the gas pump.

Tom, without looking at her, said, "Nice night out," then looked at the duffel bag. "Where you headed?"

"Arizona," she answered.

Tom frowned. She smiled. "It's west of here. My name is Salome. I'm a dancer."

Tom offered his hand. "I'm Tom."

"Pleased to meet you." She shook his hand with both of hers.

He retrieved his hand and said, "I'm going west. You want a lift?"

"Sure." Salome grabbed her duffel bag and walked around the pump and rolled the bag into the bed of the pickup. "Say, Tom?"

Tom removed the nozzle. "What?"

"That's not a body under the tarp, is it?"

Tom chuckled and replaced the nozzle. "No, that's not a body. I don't kill people anymore."

"That's good to know," she said and walked around the back of the pickup. Tom got in and unlocked the passenger door. Salome hopped in. "Wagons ho," she said. Tom nodded agreement.

About twenty miles down the highway, Salome was asleep. Tom saw a sign that read Stillwater River. He took the exit and parked near a bridge. Salome stirred. Tom opened the compartment behind his door, got the bag of guns, stepped out of the pickup, and eased the door closed. Salome sat up a little in the seat and watched Tom walk to the bridge. As he stepped onto the bridge, she rolled down the window and leaned out so she could see better. Tom reached in the bag and gripped a 45. He set the bag near the edge of the railing and then heaved the weapon out over the river. It splashed in. He sent the other weapon arching out over the river, and heard it splash. He put the money pouch from the bag into his coat pocket, then tore the bag in half and dropped it over the railing. He took a step back and sighed.

When he turned toward his truck he saw Salome watching him. He met her gaze, and walked back to the truck. They looked at each other.

Salome said, "Whatever you threw in the river sounded awful heavy."

"You have no idea."

"Where the hell are we, anyway?"

"I'm not exactly sure." Tom backed the truck around and started toward the bridge.

"So, tell me about yourself, Tom."

"What?"

"Tell me everything. It's a long way to Arizona."

Tom took a deep breath and exhaled as they crossed the bridge. "You wouldn't understand. Besides, I don't want to talk about it."

Salome leaned forward and looked at Tom. The way he stared out at the world reminded her of her grandfather, who was in the VA hospital in Prescott, Arizona. She sat back in her seat, settled her shoulder against the passenger side door and stared out the window. Before another hour had passed he stopped for coffee.

When he came out of the convenience store he saw Salome getting into a van. She reached out to close the van door and glanced over at Tom's pickup. He waited for her to turn away, knowing she would continue her journey without him. He felt there was something wrong about that. He saw her close the van door, not as if he were watching a movie, but as if he were in a movie watching real life. When the van was gone he looked at the ground and walked to his truck. He was eager for the road.

Homecoming

March 1970: Freeland, Indiana

Tom Warden had been back from Vietnam for two months and was currently attending Indiana University in Bloomington, Indiana. He had used the mail to register for the spring semester at Indiana University during his last month in Nam. He went back to college because that was the plan when he was drafted, and he had no other plan. It was a plan made in a more rational time, a plan that continued where he left off before going to war. It made sense just to skip the last two years of his life, especially the last year. Just chalk it up as a mistake—forget it, like it never happened. He wanted to want that, but couldn't.

Tom came to the farm for the weekend to see his mother and father. He was sitting at the kitchen table eating cereal with his father. He had a sense of needing to do something, and then he felt like he didn't really have to do anything. He felt like a fish out of water, a man without a country, without a home; like he didn't belong. Well, maybe belong, but didn't want to. He was welcomed as the man he used to be, not who he was now. Tom inhabited the body of a stranger. He had to remember who that man was so he could act like that man again. Keep the disguise up so no one would discover the Tom they knew was not inside. He looked out the kitchen window at the cornfield. Tiny drifts from an earlier snowfall formed around the corn stalks left behind by the corn picker. He wanted to be out there. It occurred to him to go pheasant hunting. If this were before the war, he would go pheasant hunting. He felt an urge to just walk through the fields. The harvested fields reminded him of rice paddies in the dry season. A harvested field had the same look for Tom no matter what the country. He wanted to be out there walking. He wanted out.

Tom got up from the table with his cereal bowl and went to the sink to rinse it. As he walked toward the basement door, his father said, "I'm sorry about you and Shirley. I thought you'd been through enough and now this." Tears welled up in his father's eyes.

"It's OK, Dad. I half expected it. Anyway, I don't think it would be a good idea for me to get married right now." Tom looked down and turned for the basement stairs, not waiting for acknowledgment or a response. He did not feel capable of explaining a feeling he did not fully understand. There was just no way he could be married. It was hard enough being in the same room with anyone for more than a few minutes. Tom escaped down the stairs and into the basement. He wanted to be out there, walking.

He took his father's shotgun from behind the furnace room door where it always was. He took the box of #8 shot 12-gauge shotgun shells from the shelf. He put five or six rounds in his coat pocket while it was still hanging on the hook, where he had left it two years ago. He put the coat on and tried to think of what that other man would do. He tried to feel what that other man had felt two years ago. It wasn't any use.

He didn't feel who he was, now or then. All Tom felt was an almost uncontrollable urge to walk through the fields with a weapon. His cover was that he was going pheasant hunting, like he had always done, but this was entirely different. What Tom knew for sure is that he was going to walk out into the empty fields with a loaded weapon. Then he would feel normal, feel OK, almost safe. Nothing more, nothing less.

Tom picked up the shotgun and broke it open to check the chamber. Empty. *Always clear your weapon while in base camp if you aren't in a bunker facing the wire.* He left the basement, trying not to think. He wanted to stop, not give in to the morbid urge, but he was just plain tired of trying to make the feeling go away. He wondered why the obsession was so strong. He knew he shouldn't be giving in to the sensations he had in a combat zone but was too beaten to resist. *What difference does it make, anyway?* He could walk through the fields with his weapon, like on patrol, and everyone would think he was out hunting like a normal young man of his age and background. Tom walked up out of the basement into the garage and across the gravel driveway. He cradled his weapon with his left arm, passed between the barn and corn crib, then out into the fields.

He did not use this time to go over his plans for the future, a future he did not really believe was there. He got to the edge of the field and turned right, toward the road a quarter of a mile away. He walked parallel to the rows of fallen cornstalks. Here and there he could see crows cleaning up the small, half-formed ears of corn left behind by the picker. He felt surrounded by the cold. There was a light wind, just enough to make the snow hiss through the corn shucks. Tom thought of the fox den down around the creek at the edge of the farm and how a crow had once gotten caught in a fox trap he set. Tom remembered how that crow had nearly bitten through his leather glove when he released it. Now the crows seemed menacing. They flew past and looked at him like they knew he was the one who trapped crows. Tom kept walking and walking. No thoughts. That was the best part—no thoughts.

He neared the fence line along the road. He uncradled the 12-gauge and carried it at the ready position. He knew the pheasants would flush when he got to the fence line where they hid. The pheasants would usually wait in the tall grass as long as they felt safe, then burst into the air. He made it all the way to the fence, but no game showed itself. He turned left along the fence toward the creek, then left at the creek away from the road, deeper into the fields. He followed the creek all the way to the south fence that separated the home place from the McAfee farm. He then plodded toward the southeast corner of the farm where the fence met the road. The sun was a little higher. Tom figured it was about 10:30 am. It felt colder.

Whenever he started to think, he caught himself and just watched the ground, looking for the tracks left by the tractor and corn picker. The crows were keeping their distance now. As he approached the road, keeping next to the fence line, he automatically got ready for the pheasants to flush, and they did. Three of them. Tom stopped and watched them. Two flew close together, veering to his left. One flew almost straight away from him into the cover across the road. It took about two heartbeats, then Tom realized he hadn't fired his weapon. Something that was instinctive hadn't happened.

Back when he was in high school, he would have snapped the gun up and fired before he thought about it. He probably would have gotten both pheasants on the left with one shot. Tom was very good with a shotgun. He broke open the shotgun and removed the shells, putting them in his pocket, leaving the breach of the weapon opened and cradled in his left arm. Tom got up on the gravel road and started making his way back to the farmhouse.

His thoughts were anything but clear. Did he hold his fire because he had lost the killer instinct? Not shooting seemed to have been a choice made before the moment of truth when the pheasants flushed. Was it just apathy? Just part of the non-reaction, the obsessive separation, the attitude of, *If it's not trying to kill me I'm not interested.* It was true that if it wasn't a threat, it wasn't important to him. Tom wanted to believe he held his fire and let the pheasants live because he was a noble and good man, but that just wasn't the whole story. *How could not killing make up for all his other killing?* He could measure the killing. The not-killing would forever be an unknown quantity.

It was near noon. The wind had picked up and was blowing cold in his face. At this distance, the brick farmhouse Tom grew up in only looked familiar. He couldn't shake the feeling that he had only seen it in a photograph and didn't really know what or who was inside. He wanted to keep walking toward the house without ever reaching it, but, of course he did arrive at the house and went back in through the basement door.

He put his father's shotgun back behind the furnace room door. After replacing the shells in the box on the shelf, he hung up his coat on the same hook where he had always hung it. It still felt like another man's coat and the hook didn't seem as high. He went up to the kitchen. His mother and father were just sitting down to lunch. There was a place set for him and he sat there like he always had. No one said much. Tom began to feel like everything would be all right. Like things could be the way they were. They finished lunch. His mother got up and went to the stove.

His father said, “Well, I’d better get to work.”

“Working on the corn picker?” Tom said.

“Yep. New gathering chains. Want to have it ready for next fall.”

“I’ll be out later, Dad.”

“Yep.”

His mother came back to the table with her coffee, “See you at supper, Matt?”

“Yep.”

Catherine set her cup of coffee down and rested her fingertips on the oak table.

As his father left the kitchen, Tom looked up and said, “I’m OK, Mom.”

“I was worried about you last night. Did you have a dream?”

“No…no, I don’t think so. Not anything I remember.”

“Well…”

“Really, Mom, I’ll be OK.”

“It’s just that I heard you last night.”

“Heard me? Must have been the wind.”

“It was you, Tom.”

“I guess I was restless.”

“I heard you scream. You yelled, ‘No! No!’ and something else. I came upstairs to your room. You were standing up in bed. Panting. Looking at something. I was afraid to wake you up. You finally laid down. I pulled the covers over you. You folded yourself up and covered your face with your hands."

Her fingers curled, forming fists, which she placed against her stomach. She lowered her head, then sat down. Tom stared out the kitchen window at the walnut tree.

At last he said, "I don't remember dreaming."

"Maybe you should see someone, Tom."

"See who? Tell them what? I just need some time."

"OK, Tommy. Just remember to ask for help if you need it."

"OK, Mom. I will," Tom lied. He didn't know why, but he felt there was no help. He had gone to Father Whitman, the parish priest, in his first week back from Nam. When he started talking to the priest about the things he had seen and done in combat, the priest panicked and claimed he wasn't qualified to help. He didn't give Tom a reference, not even the suggestion of who could help.

Tom nearly ran from the rectory. God's representative on earth had just told him, "I can't help you." He believed he could get through this himself. He believed he was a man and could handle it. Sitting at the kitchen table with his mother, though, he got the feeling nothing would ever be all right again. It was almost impossible to concentrate.

"You're coming to church tomorrow?"

"Sure, Mom, I'll go to church with you."

"Do you go to church in Bloomington?"

"No, Mom. I don't go to church any more." He looked over at his mother and shrugged his shoulders.

His mother took a sip of coffee and said, "They say there are no atheists in fox holes." Her voice dropped slightly at the end.

"There were no priests, either, Mom." He scooted his chair away from the table and started to get up. Then sat back down with his elbows on his knees. "Father Whitman wouldn't or couldn't help." Tom looked at the palms of his hands and continued. "I don't know…the Catholic Church just seems irrelevant right now, Mom. Not your fault, but…I don't feel close to its God either. I want to hide from that God. The one who burns people in hell for eternity. Doesn't seem fair somehow."

* * *

Catherine Warden watched her son draw in a breath. When he let it out, to her it seemed that it was his last. She waited. The *tick tock* from the grandfather clock seemed to stop time more than mark it. The one o'clock chime seemed unfair. Tom stirred in his chair, then raised himself up.

"I'm going out to help Dad."

"You'll be in for supper?"

"Sure, Mom, I'll be in for supper."

Catherine stood and watched her son go out the kitchen door and close it carefully behind him. She sat down and put her face in her hands. *Tommy is gone,* she thought, *and he's never coming home*. She had seen it happen to her brother and the boys she knew in high school. It had happened to Wilfred, the World War I veteran, who hauled grain and lived alone. Her tears were not just for her son, but also for all who carried the pride and shame of being a good soldier – The silent men who made secret choices.

SOLDIER FOR ALL SEASONS

I must get closer to the bone,
cut deep, not stay my hand,
so you can understand the anguish,
of the soldier in the sand.

It was my choice, my heart's desire,
so please don't get me wrong.
When I heard the call to arms,
I gladly went along.

Yet I want to blame the ones who sent me,
made me feel like damaged goods.
I want them to feel the horror
of the soldier in the woods.

I fought my war for freedom,
to keep the home fire safe.
I came back from Vietnam,
to find I had no place.

I want America to know,
combat did not break my will.
In the end it was the sadness,
of the soldier on the hill.

When a nation sends its best to war,
to show the power it can wield,
I want all to know the price that's paid
by the soldier in the field.

A soldier's family knows too well,
the grief that has been sewn.
They stand beside, but cannot touch,
their soldier home alone.

When you raise the call to war,
no matter what the reasons,
In the end, you break the heart,
of the soldier for all seasons.

Glossary

AO: Acronym for *area of operation.*

APC: Acronym for *armored personnel carrier.* A tracked vehicle used to transport a squad of infantry.

ARVN: Acronym for *Army Republic of Vietnam.*

boo-coo: From the French word beaucoup, meaning many or much.

Charlie: The shortened slang term for VC (Victor Charlie) or Vietcong guerrillas fighting against the South Vietnamese government and the American armed forces.

CP: Acronym for *command post.*

di di mau: The literal translation from Vietnamese is *go, go quickly.* American slang would be, *get out of Dodge.*

EM club: The social club for enlisted men on a military base. Enlisted men, NCOs (sergeants) and officers each had their own social clubs on a military base.

FNG: Acronym for *fucking new guy.* The slang term used when referring to any soldier newly arrived in South Vietnam.

klick: Slang for one kilometer.

Lambretas: The soldiers in Vietnam referred to all motor scooters as Lambretas because Lambreta manufactured most of them.

LAW: Acronym for *light antitank weapon.* A shoulder mounted weapon used by American troops in Vietnam.

LZ: Acronym for landing zone, which was an open area selected for inserting or extracting combat troops by helicopter.

medevac: Slang for medical evacuation. The term "dust off" was also used.

NVA: Acronym for *North Vietnamese Army.*

point: The first position of an advancing column of soldiers. The soldier walking point would likely be the first to trip a booby-trap or encounter enemy troops.

ROK: Acronym for *Republic of Korea*

RPG: Acronym for *rocket propelled grenade.* The shoulder-mounted launcher was often carried by a Vietcong or NVA soldier along with several rounds.

steel pot: Slang for the steel helmet worn by American armed forces soldiers.

slicks: The Bell UH-1 transport helicopter usually with the sliding side doors removed. The only armament was two M-60 machine guns slung or mounted in the open doorways.

VC: Acronym for *Vietcong*, referring to the guerrillas fighting against the South Vietnamese government and the American armed forces.

About the Author

Tom is the youngest of four. He grew up on a farm in Indiana with his brother and two sisters. He served as an infantry sergeant in the Vietnam War and was honorably discharged December 15th, 1969.

For the next twenty years he held jobs ranging from installing steam boilers to night manager of a clothing store.

In 1990 Tom moved to Arizona, where he began writing. He wrote for and performed in a theater troupe, which examined how violence impacts our lives. He dabbled with standup comedy, performed improvisational theatre, and acted in independent films. In 1995 he earned a B.S. in Engineering from Northern Arizona University.

He now lives in Page Springs, Arizona, where he tends his sustainable garden and continues to write.

Readers can contact the author through
http://dragontalebooks.com/

Made in the USA
Middletown, DE
23 November 2022